Memoirs of a Virus Programmer

Pete Flies

StoneGarden.Net Publishing
http://www.stonegarden.net

Memoirs of a Virus Programmer. Copyright © 2005 Pete Flies

ISBN: 0-9765426-8-4

This is a work of fiction. Names, characters, places and incidents are products of the author's imagination or are used fictitiously and are not to be construed as real. Any resemblance to actual events, locales organizations or persons, living or dead, is entirely coincidental.

StoneGarden.Net Publishing

3851 Cottonwood Dr.

Danville, CA 94506

All rights reserved. Printed in the United States of America. No part of this book may be used or reproduced in any manner whatsoever without written permission, except in the case of brief quotations embodied in critical articles and reviews. For information address StoneGarden.Net Publishing.

First StoneGarden.Net Publishing paperback printing: April 2005

First StoneGarden.net Publishing ebook printing: April 2005

Visit StoneGarden.Net Publishing on the web at http://www.stonegarden.net.

Memoirs of a Virus Programmer

/* The Invocation to Katya*/

First of all, Katya, this is not a suicide note. I don't have much time, although right now I'm very much yearning for your hand to hold for a good forty or fifty years. Maturity frightened me until it finally happened, and it arrived in the same manner that love and madness did; blindsiding. I realize now, that for the past few years I've been drowning in a three foot lake because I didn't have the sense to stand up and look around. Somehow, it seems that naivety can be as much a blessing as experience is, but I prefer the filters of experience.

Looking back on our time together, Katya, I feel that I failed to tell you many things. Therefore, I'll tell you from the beginning of all relevant memory. Like every other man and woman on earth, I could bleed out a staggering work many hundreds of pages long, but I know that you probably don't have a surplus of time to invest in memoirs from past lovers and, as I said, I am unbelievably pressed for time. I don't wish to bore you, Katya, nor tire you, so I will try to be brief; and if you've already become listless towards this paragraph, I apologize and intend to keep things moving swiftly as your reading continues, and, really, based on how much I've written already, I realize at this point that I must strike this very sentence from the story, for decorum if nothing else.

Well then, I had better get started telling, rather than meandering, for slapping down words requires no writer. I could hire a computer programmer to put words down. A programmer could design an algorithm to produce words at several gigahertz per second, or even teraflops per second by the time you read this. But, summarily, this introduction has gone on too long, and my meter is running. So here I begin, Katya, starting with my first day of employment in the real world, at the famous Beamer

Pete Flies

Corporation in Minneapolis.

Memoirs of a Virus Programmer

/* My first day at Beamer in the pervasive whir. Also my preference to be called Johnny instead of John. */

In those days, the Beamer hallways and offices seldom broke the silence. However, somewhere between nothing and noise was a 'whir,' like the sound that might be found at the end of the universe, after infinity, in the white space. A laptop computer whirred a soft noiseless noise among the sheaves of paper on my manager's desk. The manager spoke in a most genial fashion, and as he spoke, his brushy moustache bounced over his upper lip like a little floor broom at work. The vigor of the moustache led me to believe that if I tipped the manager upside down and held his legs like wheelbarrow handles, his moustache might clean anything from linoleum to hardwood.

"...Now do you prefer 'John' or 'Johnny'?" He tilted his head at me to indicate an ambitious atmosphere of listening.

I replied, "I prefer 'Johnny.' Absolutely."

The ice broke between us as we exchanged smiles, but soon the warble of my voice filtered out of the room, and the whirring monotone resumed.

My manager smiled, "Why 'Johnny' so absolutely?" as he shifted his neck to a cervical contrapposto.

I said, "'Johnny' sounds energetic, but 'John' does not. To me the sound of 'Johnny' invokes the image of an active person, whereas 'John' sounds settled, like an old man eating popcorn with his gums."

"I understand, I suppose," the manager curled his lips

completely under his moustache, "I guess that's what we all want in a way. To feel young."

<----------------------"whir."---------------------->

He continued talking to me and we shared politeness to a wonderful degree. Unto each comment came another positive comment. The score always remained zero to zero, as perhaps a game of basketball between Jesus and Buddha might play out.

"Any questions so far, Johnny?"

"Mmmmmmmmmm...none yet." To fortify my response, I nodded and smiled.

"If you think of any questions, stop me immediately. Don't be shy here at Beamer."

"I appreciate it."

"You're welcome."

"It's nice to feel welcome here at Beamer," I beamed.

"Hey, that's exactly what we want to hear. May I offer you some green tea?"

* * * * *

In the end, to our relief and tilted heads, my manager discovered that I rooted for the Minnesota Vikings football team, while he enjoyed the Green Bay Packers. I tilted my head sidelike, and made a playful but inquisitive jibe so as not to disturb the air in the four corners of the windowless office.

I said sarcastically, "You know it's sad that your quarterback must use addictive drugs to play effectively."

He said, "Likewise, it is unfortunate that the Vikings

have never won a Superbowl."

"Touche!"

"whir!"

And we laughed openly in hardy unison while we adjusted our positions in our seats. I leaned forward, then back again, crossed and uncrossed my legs, then crossed the other leg, then placed my unfolded hands on my ankle, folded them, unfolded them, and laid one hand on top of the other, peacefully. My heart beat betwixt the small talk, telling me, *"Beamer will be a fine place to become a success in this short life. This too, too remarkably short and wonderfully sweet life. Here I will not struggle like so many others my age. Here I will find a comfortable home to be creative in."* Before continuing the conversation I removed my hands from my ankle, uncrossed my legs, placed my hands on my thighs, straightened my back, and finally crossed one leg over the other.

He tilted his head and said, "Let's get through some of this paperwork right away."

I nodded amply.

He nodded back, "I'll just start trying to explain the documents while you sign them…"

I nattered, "Shouldn't I…Oh, I'm sorry…were you finished speaking?"

He tilted, "Go ahead."

I wilted, "No, go ahead. I interrupted you."

He lilted, "What was your question?"

I chuckled, "Well, perhaps if I let you finish speaking my question will be answered."

And submitting coyly, he concluded, "I was finished."

"Ah! Ok. Well, then," I said, "Before I so rudely interrupted you, I was going to ask: shouldn't I read these documents first?"

He frowned painfully. "Personally, I wouldn't. Policy says you have to read them, but you can just sign them and take them back to your office. You'll have sufficient time to read them when you get back from Chicago, because tomorrow you are flying there for orientation."

"Chicago?" I said, "I am honored." (Tilt.)

"Well, I hope you do enjoy it." (Pursed lips *a la* tilt.)

As I left, my manager added, "Welcome, Johnny. You are officially a Beamer now. Congratulations, you're part of the Team!"

"whir!"

/* The drive to the neighborhood in suburbia, under a watchful moon, where the streets have odd names, and my new roommate's dislike of tattoos. */

On I drove into the night - the first of the Beamer nights. Through my windshield the fattening crescent moon smiled in the 5:00 sky like the cheshire cat. It smiled at all the commuting angels and sinners and saints and false prophets driving around me.

In the rear-view mirror, I said to my reflection, "You did it Johnny. You *made it* here. You have reached the apple you desired by climbing the difficult branches. Even with mistakes, you've found success. But now the time to work begins. Programming days are ahead. You must stay focused and dedicated on writing quality code for Beamer. This is the real world now. No more college nights of playing the wine game or other trivial pursuits. Maybe you can retire at age fifty. Have you thought about that, Johnny?"

I hadn't.

The city traffic queued up like a colon studded with Nelson cheese. My car stuttered along as my brain conjured childhood memories of nights when I laid in the alfalfa fields basking in the moonlight, watching the nightly parade of a billion stars. The moon is always bigger and better when you never get to see it. I'm forever a daydreamer. I'm a perfect sucker for a grifter or shady salesman as long as the dreamscape sounds good, and the grass is alfalfa, and the moon big and round.

Thus the fully waxed moon summoned to me thoughts of youth. I mused on days spent with my little brother and how we lounged in the field while our bored yellow dog waited for one of us to throw a stick. The summer moon always seemed happy. The Sea of Tranquility always looked to me like a fresh cow kicking up her hooves.

But in the traffic, I lost the moon. I suddenly snapped loose of my daydreaming when the moon went behind a square billboard. The billboard displayed a picture of an unborn fetus accompanied by large block letters that read, 'Abortion is Murder'. I lost my train of daydream thought...

The traffic trudged along as I considered other advantages in life endowed to me, in terms of the pursuit of happiness. At the budding age of twenty-two, the difficulties of poverty were behind me. I would let father and my little brother worry about money on their latest dirt farm. And, good God almighty: I even took solace in thinking that I had improved upon my upbringing. Retrospect is a razor.

From Minneapolis to the suburb of my new residence, the commute took an hour during rush hour. My roommate, Jamie, insisted on moving to a neighborhood far from the Beamer building where he and I worked. When I suggested we live in the least expensive area of Minneapolis, his face turned sour.

"I am not moving to the slum," he said, "where bars and tattoo shops are everywhere. Not to mention the filth. There's too much white trash and...well, crime in general, " meaning poor black people.

I asked, "What's wrong with tattoos?"

He abruptly retorted, "What's right about tattoos?"

I reasoned, "An argument for both sides exists, I imagine."

In the end I ceded to his residential preference. I even let Jamie select the house itself since money did not matter to us. It was the glorious and apoplectic year of 2000, when the internet revolution swept the markets with unwavering optimism, when the technological advancements blew through all obstacles of person-to-person connectivity. The world teemed with the outpourings of engineering inventiveness, such as e-business, instant messaging, hand-held computing, embedded microchips, and more flavors of coffee than ever.

Being new in my neighborhood, I became lost on the naming scheme of the streets. Foolishly, I turned onto 44th Court instead of 44th Drive. My car crept around the streets in search of my house number until I realized my wrong turn, only after driving past every house on the street. I turned onto 44th Lane and randomly turned on 44th Street thinking 44th Drive might be there. The road curved repeatedly until I lost all directional bearing.

Soon enough I arrived at 44th Drive. But instead of 44th Court I needed to turn left on 43rd Street and curve along until I came to the seemingly impossible intersection of 43rd Street and 43rd Street. Then another left on 43rd Street that somehow became West Lakeside Street and then morphed to Whisper Hill Drive and finally became 44th Avenue. From 44th Avenue, to the winding 44th Court, and finally to the correct 42nd Lane.

With the car parked in the driveway, I laughed at my wrong turn that caused thirty minutes of neighborhood orientation. I sighed and said out loud to the night, "How lucky I am that every day is a learning experience."

/* How the virgin Beamer night was spent. */

Jamie, my aforementioned roommate, was not present when I arrived at home. However, he'd arranged the entire house in one day. I admired his industry and questioned my own. Prior to this moment, Jamie hadn't led on to his religiosity, but his knick-knacks and decorative selection obviated this fact. Suddenly I realized how poorly I knew Jamie Appleton. During college we had spent countless hours in the computer labs and talked of various technical topics, but regrettably he and I discussed little else.

I turned on the stereo and immediately came the outpourings of a song expounding on the merits of an awesome God, and of course His son Jesus was involved, too. A reserved, wooden cross hung on the wall. On the coffee table several books were stacked in a neat disarray to fully expose each of the titles and the authors' names. I peeked at the titles and opened each book to a random page. In the first book, I read:

"Many Christians believe the anti-Christ is alive and well in today's world. His manifestation will become apparent on the eve of the 21st century. Biblical scholars have decoded and proved that the time for rapture will occur on January 1, 2001. (Ref: Revelation 13:6-66, St. John et al, St. Paul's letters from his permanency in Circle VIII, Bolgias 6,8, and 9.)"

The topic frightened me so much that I moved on, to the next book, in which a Christian weightlifter was interviewed. This strongman traveled across the United States with his kids performing weightlifting feats, doing God's work, using God's strength to benchpress nearly 700 pounds. He had performed this feat for many audiences to convey the power God instilled - no - planted inside of him. The man dedicated himself for the kids of America:

"I am on a mission to show kids how to avoid distractions and stay focused in this journey to heaven. We as Christians must get the attention of the young people. They need to hear the message young. If we don't catch their eye, someone else certainly will. There are many souls to save from 'the terror, the pit, and the snare,' as described in Isaiah 24, the excruciating death of burning in hell."

"Uff-da!" I grunted and dropped the book. The pit and the snare sounded too horrible to go on further, and the third book awaited me. In the third book was mentioned a story of a young lady who had been saved, mended, repaired by the power of God through a medical miracle. This child had undergone several surgeries dealing with her heart and lungs. During all invasive medical procedures, her mother and father prayed continuously, except, of course, while they ate, slept, and voided waste from their clamoring bodies. The third surgery involved the most advanced techniques and instruments and educated professionals available, and through God, this team of people and equipment successfully removed a blocking tumor from an artery. The family rejoiced wholeheartedly, praising God and those saints related to surgical affairs. God's will, through the hands of the surgeon, had saved the girl. But unfortunately at the time of publication the daughter could not comment because she was still in intensive care on a respirator and a machine that regulated her circulation. Reading this account of God's mercy impressed me indelibly, for a minute or so.

I closed the books, turned off the music, and considered saying a prayer so that I would not burn in hell for all eternity. But then the door opened to reveal Jamie's pale head peering out from behind a large plant.

"Hello Johnny! Do you still recognize the place?"

"Hardly," I said, "You must have been diligent today."

"And I was assiduous - at acquiring the deciduous!"

I chuckled, "That's very clever!"

"Thank you. Where shall I put this plant?"

I said, "Anywhere you'd like, I imagine. My home furnishings are few; they consist of a TV tray and a brothel guide I bought in Reno once on spring break."

"Oh, that's so funny," said Jamie with bright eyes, "You have *got* to show me that brothel guide someday; I love traveling souvenirs. I hope you don't mind my arrangements and my clutter. My manager sent me home early today after I mentioned the need to tidy up. My manager seems really great."

"That's terrific, Jamie."

"And yours?" he said.

"My what?" I asked.

"Your day?"

"Which part?"

"Your manager."

"Yes, well, he seems fine likewise," I said. "I'm leaving tomorrow for orientation in Chicago."

He tilted his head, "Oh, nice! You are so lucky."

I tilted my head, "Thank you."

I changed my tone to a false seriousness, "Now the real question, Jamie: did you get this house wired today?"

Jamie set down his plant. "No I didn't. Can you believe that? Let's get on with it right now."

"Yes, let us," I said.

He and I eagerly mustered our computer boxes in the living room, so that we could get connected to the network.

* * * * *

I said, "Let's have a few beers while we work, in celebration."

"Oh, I'd love to!" Jamie exclaimed, "except that I don't drink," and he frowned.

"Not even one drink?" I applied peer pressure.

He apologized to me, "I'm sorry, but I abstain."

"That is an admirable habit, I suppose." I thought for an instant, then said, "I'll abstain for the night as well."

We assembled our equipment over the next hour and argued over geek-stimulating topics, jovially poking at ISP's, paradigms, API's, platforms, and databases.

I said, "You're still using that old operating system?"

"Are you kidding?" Jamie replied, "I have a partition on this machine. I run multiple versions. What are you talking about anyway? Look at your ancient monitor."

I sneered, "It's just nostalgia for the days when you're operating system actually operated."

"That's not the only one I run, let me assure you."

"Yes, then I am assured," I said, rolling my eyes in good fun.

On that first Beamer night, Jamie and I poetically shared programming stories, telling of computer lab lore, and how we wrangled in bugs that had strayed from the herd of working code. One story ventured along as so:

"This one application," I said, "which was well over a fifteen KLOC, a multithreaded C++ memory pig, jammed a hundred threads in a race condition for a semaphore with the main thread that was waiting to join. And there I sat without a clue."

"So what did you do?" Jamie asked.

"Well, I set a breakpoint and a print line every time someone nabbed the semaphore in question. Of course, wouldn't you know, someone..." et cetera.

Yes, Katya, I know - esoteric lingo dulls the stoutest audience, so I will go not further on this topic. But perforce, I must say, Jamie Appleton and I were two happy codemonkeys until late into the night on the first of the Beamer nights.

Before I went to bed that night, I happily ironed my pants for the flight to Chicago.

/* How at dinner, the Beamer businessmen decide to educate us with tales of Beamerdom. */

The plane hit the tarmac in a clattering tumult, and no sooner had I stepped into the O'Hare concourse than a Beamer human resources representative greeted me, scooped me into a cab, and showed me to a room in the Hotel Ritz. In my naivety, I asked the price of the hotel to determine what I owed her.

She winked at me, "Never mind the cost."

I demurely blushed at the extravagance of her fluttering eyelids. The woman expressed great interest in us new hires, and in mascara. She distributed a database of Beamer facts in the most upbeat and likable manner.

"Here's your itineraries and documentation for orientation. Don't lose this document or you'll be in trouble."

She paused to comb our faces with her lashing eyes, then continued, "Oh, you won't really be in trouble, we'll just give you another packet. I love joking around with you new Beamers; you are all so very impressionable. But that's good! That's good. You are all very eager and motivated, and that's exciting! Just a word of advice on the largest document inside the packet; it illustrates the conduct that Beamer requests of all employees. These are statements that help make Beamer one of the most trusted and ethical businesses in the world. In essence, the document covers all areas that concern our competitive advantage in the marketplace, and with each piece of the Team doing his or her part, Beamer can avoid unnecessary setbacks. Also, this will help your business acumen, personal development within Beamer, and how to handle business people and customers. It's a comprehensive guide to standards and behavior for you to integrate into your daily routine, which will also help you mesh seamlessly into the Team here, not only in the departmental Team, but also into the Beamer Team as a whole. The same regulations apply to all Beamers, on all Teams, so learning these regulations now is incumbent for your future ability to move from one Team to another and start being productive right away, without having to learn a new set of rules for each separate Team. We want you to be able to fit in seamlessly. You'll hear that word often from me: *seamlessly*. Doesn't it sound good? Yes?"

The new Beamers nodded shyly as she batted her heavy blue-black eyelids.

She continued, "Remember, this is an umbrella document for all Beamers, so you're not the only ones that have to read it. You're not the only unlucky ones, right? Ha Ha Ha!" she cackled.

She pointed her long, red fingernails at the document in my hand, "But most of this information will be obvious to you anyway. No drugs, no fighting, no illegal gambling. Of course, no drinking at work...shucks, right? Ha ha ha!" she cackled.

"Yes. A good deal of this information is obvious," she continued, "but we need you to sign each sheet for our records. At times Beamer will throw a Team party and they may or may not serve alcoholic beverages, so exceptions for some rules exist, although if you do attend a Beamer party, there is a limit on the number of beverages any single Beamer can consume at such events. I believe they allow two drinks per person. And of course you do not have to attend or imbibe or do anything you wish not to do. No one will force you; Beamer encourages personal decision. We respect the decision to abstain, absolutely. That's one thing you'll find here is tolerance for everyone's beliefs. We'll get to much more of this in the next few days."

In the hotel room, a note on my pillow read, "If you wish,

come downstairs for dinner at 7:00 pm. Several veteran Beamer employees will be present at dinner. The hotel has an excellent restaurant with fine cuisine from many cultures. We hope to see you there."

I ironed my pants, and then descended in the glass elevator, where I noticed a wrinkle had formed on my pants, so I returned to my room to iron the pants once again.

In college I learned many words that meant nothing to me, and whenever I felt in the presence of those words, I tried to include them in my speech as often as possible. The restaurant displayed great postmodern artwork and fineries that invited my attention, so I walked slowly around the restaurant inspecting the art until a polite woman approached me and inquired to my wandering about.

"May I help you?" she asked.

"Oh, you may," I gasped, "Ahh! This artwork," I guessed, "I so love Symbolist paintings."

"Do you? Well, this is a Matisse."

I smiled, "Ah, what a fine Symbolist he was."

"I'm sorry to tell you, he was not a Symbolist painter."

"No? Then surely an Expressionist."

"No."

"I see in the brush strokes here elements of Post-impressionism. Or actually, judging by this piece, I imagine he was sympathetic to Cubism. If not, then surely he was, indeed, an Abstract-Expressionist."

"Not at all."

"Dadaist."

"No."

"Rococo."

"That's absurd, actually," laughed the woman. I took a breath. "Well, Matisse can be nothing but a Minimalist, for what else is left? Matisse the Minimalist."

"No. I'm sorry," she said, "but he was a Fauvist."

I politely sniggered at her ignorance, "Ma'am, you do not have to apologize for Matisse's abrogation of Renaissance ideals."

"Oh Jesus," she said, in agreement, as I perceived it at the time. She went on, "May I help find you a seat?"

She directed me to a table where the newly hired Beamers sat quietly masticating on stiff bread and sipping water. I sat and joined the group in the awkward swallowing. The silence was deafening, but soon a loud group of white Beamer businessmen arrived and joined us and from that moment on, the quiet ended. An elder businessman jolted us into conversation.

"So where are you all from? Or maybe I should say, 'y'all'. Or perhaps, 'all of you', depending on what region of America you hail from." The table spilled in mirth over this anecdotal slice of American pie.

The business man put his attention around the young Beamer nearest to him and said, "How about you."

The newly hired Beamer said, "I'm from Toledo…"

"Wait!" said one of the other businessmen, "These new ladies and gentlemen have no drinks. Let's properly get them started on Beamer wages."

"Of course! Waitress - these folks need some beverages of better cheer. And I think I'll freshen up mine as well. Another gin and tonic for me, please."

"And I," said another businessman.

"And I."

"And I'll have another water," said a businessman, " As I'm driving this motley crew tonight. We had quite a night in Tuscaloosa last night."

"And Kalamazoo the night before."

And so all of us drank, and freshened our drinks and drank again, once, twice, many times over until the night felt a total success for all involved, especially me, since weakness is my strength.

The head businessman spoke loudly to us seated at the table. "Software engineers, I presume?"

Our heads bobbled in affirmation.

He said, "Oh that's great news. Can I get a loan from one of you?"

We all erupted in laughter again. One of the new engineers sitting across from me, from his own unexpected laughing fit, produced a long, wet mucous hangman on the end of his nose, which he failed to recognize for some time, and I could not take my eyes away from the dangling fluid no matter how I tried to look away.

The businessmen conversed smoothly and efficiently, joking at opportune moments and telling stories gregariously. Occasionally, a boisterous businessman would slip serious commentary into his canned response, teaching us highly craved facts. The man stated:

"I grew up in a town near Omaha, where my parents still live. Or rather, my mother still lives there. My father passed away five years ago, bless his soul," at which point he bowed his head briefly before continuing. "I went to the University in Lincoln, graduated with a Finance degree, and started at Beamer. That was over twenty years ago. Can you imagine that? I'm an old man, a dinosaur! Ha! But during that time I've gotten my MBA and moved into high-end sales, which I find exciting…and frustrating at times, given the nature of all the problems that occur. But I have a great Team. I started out here as a full-time, on-the-road salesman, and found out that it was a great career but I wanted something with slightly less traveling. I'm married and have two *great* daughters. They keep me busy, let me assure you! A <u>really</u> great wife, too. My home is in Birmingham now. Beamer transferred me there a few years ago. And basically, Beamer has given me everything I've wanted out of life, and I can only hope we can do the same for you, so you can have great Beamer career. We'll certainly try tonight, I can tell you that. Cheers!"

"Cheers!" Our glasses clinked in shrill staccato and my eyes blurred into dreamy crescents, slightly bloodshot.

As the meal ended, I pulled out my wallet to pay for my end.

A businessman said, "Whoa Johnny! Hold on a minute. Put that thing away, you're going to make the rest of us look bad." Everyone laughed again. He continued, "You're here on business. Use your Beamer credit card and expense it when you get home. If you learn to enjoy yourself, life at Beamer will fly right by. Come to think of it…I don't remember any of it."

The table burst in laughter again.

"Oh, I'm kidding. C'mon now, I'm joking…I think."

The businessmen finished their drinks and left us at the table laughing. As the animation filtered out of the room, we young Beamers remained silent and dizzy. The conversation had ended so abruptly, that all we could do was wish for another loaf of bread to occupy our mouths.

That night in the hotel I dreamed of a cackling witch who hovered over my bed, like a Succubus, watching me, trying to steal my special purpose in life. In the dream, my bed had moved to a green pasture, with me still in it. Around my bed in the pasture were amiable, puffy sheep grazing at lush patches of green grass. The witch stared menacingly at me in her hovering horror. Her partially decayed face reared back and came forward to emit a ruthlessly powerful shriek that in a jolt sheered naked each and every sheep in the pasture. The sheep immediately discontinued their grazing and blinked at me inquisitively in regard to their newfound nudeness (to which I had no explanation and felt ashamed for them).

Katya, let me tell you, my imagination frequently reached unnecessary excesses of this manner during the coming Beamer nights.

Pete Flies

/* What tragedy befell Beamer Corporation on my orientation day. */

When the alarm spurred me from my paltry hour of sleep, my tongue cried out for water and my head longed for a reason why. With my pants un-ironed, I arrived at the Beamer training facility weary, and the cheery greetings from the human resource women pierced my delicate soul.

"Good morning! Coffee is available in the rear!"

The newly hired Beamers sipped coffee and listened to more introductions and self-introductions, and introductions to speakers, and introductions to the day's scheduled events. The briefings commenced in an extremely cordial manner. Due to my nightmares I discovered myself dozing readily at the voices of the speakers but managed to glean the main idea from each half hour session.

The woman who had escorted me from the airport addressed me most often.

"Wake up Johnny! I hope we don't have to repeat all of this on account of you." She smiled and the lines in her face seared through the cake she had baked on her facial epidermis.

Upon hearing her voice I straightened up and listened intently.

"We will be administering a drug test now."

"Bowser!" I thought. To the Beamer next to me, who had a head shaped like a peanut, I said, "Good thing I've been out of college for three weeks now or this might have concluded my Beamerhood! I was very naive in college at times."

The Beamer responded, "You should still be concerned. Your eyeball's retinal fluid contains every illegal substance you've ever admitted to your body."

"Really?" I asked.

"Yes."

"But, honestly now, how would they ascertain this eyeball fluid?"

"With a needle?"

"No?"

"Yes," he nodded.

"Everything I've ever done? In my eyeball?"

"Everything," he said with conviction.

For a bit I sat silently, then decided to be silly. I said, "What about the varnishing I did in eighth grade wood shop?"

He politely scoffed, "Pfft. It's not that accurate. But maybe someday they will be able to detect such things."

I kidded, "What about any impure thoughts I've had?"

He did not answer and we peed in cups. Everyone's urine succeeded the Beamer orientation.

The human resource women continued on with fine presentations using delightful language in explaining the Beamer policies of conduct. Many documents passed under my pen that day unread but wearing my signature. To my memory I committed the fundamentals of Beamer policy:

-No sex at work.

-No jokes at work.

-No surfing at work.

-No politics at work.

-No religion at work.

-No fighting at work.

-No gambling at work.

-No tailgating at work.

-No media contact at work.

-No pandering my labor outside of work.

-No selling of my own inventions outside of work.

-No sex at work.

Before I left, the woman who'd escorted me from the airport cracked a smile and said, "Now remember this important fact: Beamer always reserves the right to modify the terms of your employment at any time based on company needs and economic status in the regional, national, and/or worldwide arenas."

We all laughed in unison because the blessed American dollar had never been so strong. We believed in the strength of the dollar. But I understood her statement well; I felt sympathetic to Beamer's struggles against those who tried to stifle Keynesian-Smithian-Reagonian economics, and promote anti-business agendas, such as the honorific Veblenites and the godless Social-Commune-Trotskyite-Democrat-Sickheads.

She went on, "Keep in mind that business changes happen rapidly, and to be a part of the Beamer team, you need to always have the environment in perspective."

A Beamer joked, "That sounds ominous."

The human resource woman started to cackle, and she made an attempt to lean on a table with her arm, but she missed the table entirely and her body toppled forward only to fracture her face on the tabletop. She slumped to the carpet.

"Gasp!"

We all gasped in terror and rushed to help her however inadequately software engineers could. I noticed a large smudge on the table where her face had made impact.

A man stepped forward and said, "I used to be a paramedic! Quick, someone call for help." Another human resource woman dialed her cell phone for emergency help and she started swearing soon after she dialed.

"This G-D phone doesn't get F service here!" she said, surprising me with her language. She became terribly vulgar for a human resource woman and I considered writing a complaint.

I asked rather intensely, "Why no service?!"

"It's this F room! I'll run outside and try."

The Beamer paramedic stooped over the injured woman and exclaimed, "She's stopped breathing!" Thus the people in the room gasped again and more fearfully.

In a matter of seconds the man determined that the injured woman lacked a pulse as well, and he cried out, "Her heart has stopped! Please, someone get the electronic defibrillator!"

Beamers scrambled throughout the building scouring the halls for a defibrillator and returned triumphant. The paramedic furiously pumped her chest and administered breaths but to no avail. He applied the defibrillator to her exposed breast and the machine read: "APPLY SHOCK NOW." Sweat beads glittered on every forehead in the room, our fears electrified the air, our common desperation for life culminated when our heroic Beamer paramedic pushed the button that applied the shock to save the Beamer human resource woman. He pushed the button.

She immediately died.

Great wailings and sobs burst forth after that, well merited wailings and sobs, of course.

When the ambulance arrived the paramedics managed to determine that our Beamer paramedic, who worked so gallantly, had lied in saying, "Her heart stopped!" The paramedics said that the shock given to the woman was what in fact had killed her. They accused the Beamer paramedic of negligence based on his expertise in the field of emergency medicine. But our valiant Beamer paramedic objected over and over.

He cried out, "Her breathing had stopped! Her heart had stopped!"

One of the newly arrived paramedics fished the dead woman's tongue out from her throat and said, "Look. She had just choked on her gum when her head hit the table. She was only unconscious from choking," and he threw the gum to his partner, "Check that out, Lou."

And Lou said figuratively, "Well...I'll be sheep-dipped in sh..."

Flabbergasted, the Beamer paramedic objected until his voice went hoarse, "But the defibrillator said to shock her! The machine is never wrong."

Lou said, "You are still negligent in even applying the

machine. Maybe her heart had stopped for a second, but my money says her heart was beating when you shocked her."

"But I had checked her pulse!"

The police arrived and asked to see the Beamer paramedic's identification, then asked to see his wrists upon which they placed handcuffs, and his face turned to stone at that moment. He was slowly led out the door to the waiting squad car.

The victim of negligence lay motionless with her plastic smile still in place, now looking much like the sad clown. The other human resource women huddled in grief. One of the women offered no support to the horrified negligent Beamer. The rest of us stood in silence as our almost-hero left.

"You fool! You idiot!" the angry human resource woman cried out so that our paramedic might hear her opinion. He was so stunned that he could not move his tongue, but his feet, on the other hand, continued the slow waltz to the exit.

I added an additional policy to my list:

-No negligence.

As for me and the other Beamers, we had to take a cab to the airport and pay the cab driver out of our pockets. One of my new Beamer mates said, "We'd better get reimbursed for this cab ride."

And another one said, "No doubt. Especially after witnessing that shocking trauma. No pun intended."

I bitterly protested their caustic commentary by frowning at the window in silence.

On the plane, I slept, and there the witch visited me in my dreams once again, this time wearing a mesh shawl that poorly covered her festering and rotting wounds. The naked sheep huddled under a tree away from her, but once again she reared her head back and came forward with the most heinous sound ever emitted or imagined, which noise motivated the naked sheep to climb into the branches of the tree and slump their bodies prostrate in fear. The sheep looked at me from their gangly perches but dared not bleat, careful not to draw the attention of the terrible whore. (And again I was overcome with shame in doing nothing for the sheep but observing.)

Memoirs of a Virus Programmer

/* The etymology of the Pepper family. Also, the Soldier of Bastogne. */

The next morning in Minneapolis, in the persistent whir of Beamer, my manager fiddled with his laptop computer.

"Just a minute, Johnny. I just downloaded the latest version of this web browser and for some reason it's not cooperating. Isn't that the norm, eh? Maybe you can come and take a look at this."

Eagerly I wheeled my chair to his side of the desk and viewed his inoperable browser.

"You've rebooted?"

"Yep."

"No install problems? The new version is compatible with Beamer software?"

"Yep."

"Have you installed Microsoft fix-pack MXXLIVCL?"

"It's the newest one available this week. It's just dead."

So it goes. We rebooted, waited, downloaded, waited, uninstalled, waited, rebooted, waited, waited, reinstalled, waited, and rebooted with minimal speaking. Once the browser worked properly I wheeled my chair back to its original position.

The manager pulled out a sheet of paper and recorded the date, time, and my name.

"What kind of name is Johnny Pepper? I mean, where does the name 'Pepper' come from in the world?"

I said, "I believe it is Irish-Mestizo-Moroccan. And Norwegian."

"Irish-Mestizo-Moroccan! I've never heard of such a genealogic soup. But it must have a single origin, no?"

"In a sense. My ancestor Paddy O'Reilly escaped Ireland to work in Mexico but found only starvation in a peon enclave, where he was an obvious minority of one. When little hope remained, he gained work on a commercial ship that set voyage for Morocco. On one particular trip, as the story goes, Paddy became recklessly in love with a young maiden in Morocco and his ship left him behind. Paddy's high temperament and lovesickness brought him into a duel to win this woman away from her family, but before the duel, Paddy became rum drunk in a canoe while pondering his crumbling fate, and he floated to the mouth of the river and then out into the vast sea, completely unaware of his surroundings."

"Goodness!" My manager wrote a few notes on the piece of paper.

"Yes, and in the sea Paddy cursed his recklessness for losing his lover. Soon he passed out from dehydration and unbearable shame; he floated aimlessly for some time, and his thirst nearly overcame him until on the third day when a pirate vessel with a Moroccan captain sidled up next to his canoe and hoisted him aboard. The sailors slapped him fiercely but Paddy did not wake until they rubbed a large quantity of ground black pepper into each of his bulbous nostrils. Then they forced him to swab the deck and act the slave in trade for a safe return to New Orleans, Louisiana. In New Orleans, Paddy fled the ship and discovered a new lifestyle. He declared his name Paddy Pepper (as christened by the Moroccan captain), he became a gambler and followed a troupe of black musicians throughout Louisiana, searching for card games and suckers. One card game caused Paddy to flee Louisiana. Two men at the table owed money to

Paddy after a night of poker and they agreed to pay Paddy's bar tab, but they reneged. So Paddy issued two hot bullets to each of their chests. In response to this development, Paddy left that very night to ascend the Mississippi River, and he made it to the north by playing poker against the rough longshoremen stationed in every town up and down the banks of the river. When Paddy finally arrived in St. Paul, he looked considerably different due to three fresh scars gained in disagreements with various longshoremen, but always the hardy adventurer, Paddy went forth and promptly bedded a buxom betrothed Norwegian waitress and together they carried on a torrid love affair, and thus produced a healthy pregnancy. However, before Paddy's twin sons were born, an Irish policeman in St. Paul arrested Paddy for dodging the Civil War draft. Given the option of prison or enlistment, Paddy asked to be assigned to the Louisiana regular militia, which comment so angered the policeman that a charge of treason was pinned on Paddy. Fortunately for Paddy, he was not yet a United States citizen, and could hardly betray a nation he was not a member of. So instead of prosecution, the dutiful policeman immediately made Paddy a citizen and processed his Union Army papers. Of course the Army brought more adventure to Paddy, in a sense, where he went on to fight in several campaigns and earned the honor and privilege of killing a Confederate officer, then being shot accidentally by a soldier of his own regiment. Laying with his wounds on the overrun field, Paddy was captured and dragged off to Andersonville prison, where, of course, he died after a long bout of chronic dysentery."

"Goodness! Is that all?"

I smiled, "I believe so. And let me add that I admire his life immeasurably. Except for the dysentery."

"Whew," said the manager, "I'm not so sure I envy such a tumultuous ride of life."

"Yes, perhaps it would be too much for one man's life."

My manager jotted more notes as I waited in the whir and observed his moustache.

I asked, "What are you writing down?"

The moustache jittered, "As a manager I am required to note every meeting and exchange that takes place between myself and employees."

"Why's that?" I asked.

"To increase personal communication, business efficiency, and you know - legal reasons. With this documentation we have recourse for any litigation that might come our way regarding harassment or workplace issues."

"Ah! I see what you mean," I nodded. "Isn't it sad we have to safeguard ourselves in such a way?"

He sighed and tilted his head. "A necessary evil, I suppose."

The whir returned to the room. My manager diddled his pen on his desk and then looked up pensively. "Your story of Paddy got me thinking. I have a story as well. Since you were so forthcoming, I feel that I should share one. Do you mind?"

"Please go on."

"Well, my father was a World War II veteran," bounced the moustache. "But before the war he lived a common and healthy life in Wisconsin's Chippewa Valley. He built houses and raised five young children, including myself. We lived a pleasant life. Until 1941. In 1941, as you know, the United States joined the war and, like your ancestor, conscription took my father to the front as a participant. He had an excellent work ethic and made Sergeant First Class after his first major battle. I may also note that most of the men in his unit perished in that battle. However, when his unit had time off, my father concentrated on the upcoming warfare. The other soldiers flounced in brothels and bars, but my father stayed in garrison to hone his skills. In Bastogne, the Allies met an incorrigible German artillery division intent on displacing the Americans in the forest. After a week, it was my father's turn to go forward and replace a tattered and mangled Company who'd been reduced to a mere squad of men by the German artillery layoff. A Colonel assembled the men of my father's Company for a fine dinner before sending them up to the meat-grinder. In an unrehearsed rousing speech the Colonel said, 'At all costs, hold the ground, as God desires it so for Charlie Company! Dig in for Charlie Company!!' Most of the men found this speech humorous because the Colonel made a similarly inflated and uninspiring speech for all events, from shining boots to scrubbing pots, but my father took his words quite seriously, as he was a man with a great notion of duty. So in the Bastogne forest, my father dug foxholes ambitiously while the other men grumbled at the scenery of bloody craters and frozen earth. The soldiers knew that the random shrapnel selected men to die without considering their sense of duty, wealth, piety, good looks, or rank. Shrapnel is an equalizer."

My manager paused for a moment and adorned a look on his face like he was constipated. He continued, "Over the course of three weeks the shelling rattled them continuously. Every chance my father had, he worked on his foxhole. Every break in the shelling, he dug and dug. His journal disclosed a harrowing loss of sanity. He kept digging and digging, not knowing what else to do. Charlie Company grew continuously smaller as foxholes became vacant via death, so my father would move into these spaces and start digging the holes deeper. The other men scolded him for this absurd occupation. In my father's journal he describes pulling dead bodies out of the foxholes in order to commence digging."

I said, "That's very sad. The loss of life must have desensitized him…"

"So it seems. He remained alive due to this continuous and proud digging while many others died. But in the process, he started to disregard the lives of his fellow soldiers. His last journal entry read something like, 'I must maintain this position. I must maintain this position,' over and over. Soon enough, the Captain in charge of the Company was relieved of his command by a hot eight inch piece of shrapnel. My father was the highest ranking man alive. He assumed command, and soon afterward, my father carried out field executions based on the Uniform Code of Military Justice. He had to shoot soldiers who refused to follow orders. Certain lazy soldiers simply failed to maintain discipline so he relieved them of duty permanently. This did not go over well at all."

I said, "Oh my. Executions? How could he follow the rules in such a strange time?"

"Yes, well, duty is duty, even if deranged."

I said, "I doubt I could do such a thing."

"It is a shame such things must be done for freedom. I also believe the fear of mutiny, and fear of the Colonel's wrath, haunted him more than pulling his pistol trigger. In the end, all he could write in his journal revolved around hard work and 'to hell with those who didn't!' In the final day of shelling, after my father had spooned out as much earth as possible, a shell landed squarely on his foxhole and shredded him. However, he received several posthumous medals for his hard work, and the Colonel made high praises about my father being a great asset to Charlie Company."

I asked, "Did they all die in Charlie Company?"

"No. Not all of them. Right after my father's death, a

fresh Lieutenant took control and went forward with the Company and new replacements fresh off the boat."

"That's a very sad story."

"And there are many like it in wars. But winning is paramount. Imagine the alternative."

"I can't imagine." I looked down at my feet feeling glad to be safe in the peaceful world of Beamer.

My manager sensed the quiet in the room and cleared his throat. He said, "But rather than trade stories of outrageous misfortune all day, let me take you on a tour of the Beamer site and buildings."

* * * * *

With that we rose to leave, but in doing so bumped into each other at the doorway.

"After you," he said.

"No, after you," I said.

"Please."

"Age before beauty," I joked.

"I insist."

"Go on then."

"Ok, I'll go on insisting."

"Oh, well thank you then."

We guffawed a giggle and I allowed my hip to release a step forward.

/* My astonishment at the girth of Beamer, and the introduction to the office-mate. */

Meandering through the hallways, I asked my manager, "I'm not quite clear on what my primary job will be here."

My manager said, "Didn't I mention it?"

"Yes, sort of, but not very clearly. You've mentioned I'll be on the debugging team using several of the newest programming languages."

"That's correct."

I asked, "But what does that mean exactly?"
"Well, I'll have to check with a few people, but I believe you will be your own Team."

"My own Team!" I gaped.

"Yes. Here is the lunchroom."

The hallway opened into a large pavilion, perhaps better described as a gymnasium. Quickly we passed through the center of the lunchroom and I continued on with my questioning.

"How many people work here?"

"Five thousand or so. In the 1980's we had many more."

"What happened?"

He shrugged, "The market shifted and Beamer required a skills rebalancing to stay alive. Here's the Beamer convenience store. It has everything you'll need for snacks and souvenirs."

"Is that so?"

"It is."

He turned a corner and moved to the far right side of the hall to avoid a scooter traveling toward us.

I said, "I guess you have to be quick on your toes around here, huh?"

"That's for sure," he nodded.

"Is scooter traffic normal here?"

"Only for the maintenance crews. Look up at the ceiling in the hallways; it looks like spaghetti. We have a million wires and cords networking this building. Here is the Beamer bank."

"A bank, too?"

"Here is the daycare."

"Daycare?"

"Here is the massage parlor."

"Massage parlor..."

"Here is the barber."

"I had no idea."

"And here is the beauty salon."

Beamer truly had everything needed to survive and I started to wonder where all the computers stayed, but soon we journeyed through another long hallway and entered a door that revealed a room the size of a football field packed with thousands of whirring machines.

"WHIR."

Ubiquitous wires lay slathered in the pathways between the computers. Through large vents in the floor, forced air was thrust upward between our legs in an effort to keep the machines cool. Beamer employees walked slowly to and fro carrying paper in their hands, carrying CDs and diskettes. A thousand monitors blinked with data and hungry cursors. Above each monitor hung a name. A name for each computer. The names read:

-Chalupa-

-SlayedTheSlayer-

-Gandalf-

-AleutianAcrobat-

-TinyDancer-

And so on.

I had to speak loudly to overcome the noise of rushing whirs. I asked my manager, "WILL I HAVE MY OWN SERVER, TOO?"

My manager said, "No. The various department Teams have servers. Team members have to share."

"WHAT?"

He moved closer to me and repeated his statement.

I argued, "But you said I am my own Team. Is there an exception for me?"

"It's true, you will be your own Team, but you will have to work with other Teams."

"What kind of bugs will I work on?"

"A series of challenging ones dealing with our product."

"On which Beamer product?"

"Beamer <u>WebCutter</u>."

His terse answers disheartened my questioning, so I stopped. He walked all the way through the giant computer lab and opened another door that led back to my office. At the end of the tour he showed me a windowless, puny space that I would share with another Beamer. An unnatural feeling washed over me. My manager introduced me to my office with a lackluster "Ta-da," and inside sat a man named Danny, who had a peanut shaped head, a peanut shaped body, a receding hairline, and a deep dimple in his chin.

"Danny, this is Johnny," said my manager.

I extended my hand, "Hello, Danny."

Danny spoke sarcastically as he gave me a dead-fish handshake. He said, "So this is the new guy? You can't find another place for him?"

My manager replied, "Sorry Danny, this is the only office we could add another person to. And I would hate to see you get lonely."

Danny eyed me with smugness. I stood uncomfortably in the doorway and harbored my first pessimistic judgments.

"Lonely?" Danny said with a sneer to the manager, "The size of this office isn't big enough to express an emotion. But I suppose I'll let him stay." Danny's responses came off as burdens to my ear, and therefore humorless.

The three of us said nothing more until my manager bid his farewell. I sat in my chair and turned on the computer that awaited me. A wave of excitement enveloped me as I dreamed of the adventures of programming that lay ahead in the coming weeks and months. Here at Beamer in this very seat, I imagined, I'd solve problems and design software that could change the world of computing…

I was interrupted in my fantasy by Danny who had turned around to watch me.

"You'll want to set up your network password right away. You probably won't be able to figure it out, so let me show you." When he spoke, puffs of his breath hit my neck and I shuddered. I backed away from my keyboard to give Danny access.

As he created my password, I asked Danny, "How long have you worked on Beamer WebCutter, Danny?"

He mumbled, "Too long. Two years. Listen, before you get started on anything, let me give you a piece of advice. This is my golden rule: never fix other people's code unless forced. If they wrote it, let them fix it. If you think I'm going to sit here and spend my time on other people's code, you are wrong." As he spoke, he performed a gesticulating routine, and for as long as I shared the office with him, he carried out this method of social interaction wherever he went. His hands started apart in front of him, with the fingers spread, as if he held a beach ball. Then he slowly joined his fingertips in front of him as if he held a football. Then he held one hand out with his palm up as if waiting for a bird to land upon it. At points of emphasis in his dialogue, he switched from beach ball to football to bird.

I was taken aback by his golden rule. "Why would you say that? Someone must fix the code regardless of who wrote it, correct? Aren't we all a Team?"

With a beach ball he said, "If you want to disagree with me, feel free," and then a football, "What would I know, I've only been here two years now," and in conclusion he waited for a bird, "Soon enough you'll learn this truth if you're not too dense."

"And what is your job here?" I asked.

"I'm a software engineer," with a beach ball.

"Excellent! That's my title, too."

"We all have that title here, you newbie," Danny scoffed, "Everyone in this department, except the manager and the secretary, is a software engineer."

I said, "How can it be? What about those folks that test the software? What about the administrators, and the operators?"

With a beach ball he said, "They are all software engineers, every one of them," with a football, "Or of course some of us are called Designers, Developers, and Architects," and waiting for a bird, "But mostly it means nothing but 'glorified programmer.' The titles have grown from some kind of euphemistic tumor spawned by social climbers. Half of us should be called desk jockeys or spreadsheet babysitters."

"Well, then, what do you do here, Danny?"

With a beach ball, "I merge code written by our sister department in San Francisco," with a football, "All code is merged into our copy of the Beamer WebCutter code," and waiting for a bird, "Of course, every two weeks they write a stream of new code that must be merged, and every two weeks beyond that they change it all, and I begin again."

"Is it difficult?"

"It can be. We have dual maintenance on the code."

"And what is that?"

With a beach ball, "Oh, come on. Didn't you learn that in college? It means that San Francisco Beamers keep their code on servers that we cannot access here in Minneapolis," with a football, "It's a waste. If we all worked on the same servers, we'd have no need to merge it all every two weeks," and waiting for a bird, "This department is largely a sham. Beamer loves to waste money and drive my stock down."

"A sham, huh," I doubted, "I don't believe that. Beamer would not waste money like that, would they? Will you show me how your job of merging works?"

Danny groaned and turned around in his chair. He had several web browsers open to the Internet, to news stories and stock quotes, blatantly disregarding Beamer's policies that I'd learned about. He showed me his task that occupied his day; his entire job consisted of cutting-and-pasting code from one file to another.

"That's basically what I do," he said. "Of course, there's much, much more to it. You can run into many problems when this merged code compiles for the first time. That's my area of expertise."

At that moment his web browser popped up with a message telling him that he'd lost a bet placed on a major league baseball game. Danny was gambling at work, which violated another of Beamer's policies.

"Ugh!" he said, "How did the Brewers win that game?"

I grew suspicious of Danny and his motivation to succeed. He seemed perfectly superfluous with his questionable occupation and bumptious violation of Beamer policy. Without a doubt, I needed a role model, and that role model thankfully poked his head into our diminutive office at that instant.

/* How impressed I felt to be around Ted, who was a Beamer's Beamer. */

The man peering in the doorway said, "You must be the new guy. Johnny Pepper, is that right?"

I nodded. He continued, "It's a shame that I don't get over to this end of the building more often. In fact, I haven't seen Danny in a long while - how have you been, Danny?"

Danny sighed with great effort and said, "They keep paying me, so I keep coming."

"Isn't that the truth," chuckled the man in the doorway, "No matter what I do, they just keep paying me. Well, Johnny, let me introduce myself; my name is Ted. If you have time right now, why don't you follow me over to my office so we can hash over a few things."

As I turned out the door to leave, Danny said, "Hey Johnny - you left your computer unsecured. But don't bother yourself; let me get it for you. Let me take care of it for you."

"Don't be too hard on him now, Danny," Ted said, and I stifled a small urge to lunge at and throttle Danny.

Ted and I meandered down different hallways until we arrived at Ted's busy, unkempt office. His office tripled the size of my office and had two large pane windows. He had four computers whirring on his desk.

Ted said, "After fifteen years I finally was 'awarded' this office. I don't know if you know this, but Beamer uses office space as a form of promotion. After five years of employment, you get to share a bigger office, and after ten years you share an office with a window. But an office like this one is still hard to get, even if you wait twenty years. Timing is everything."

I asked, "So you've been here fifteen years?"

"Actually, I've been here longer than that. Ever since I graduated from college I've been in this neck of Beamerdom. I've worked on many, many projects. Some good ones, some bad ones. Of course, many ugly projects. Software can be such a mess when you first begin a project, or pick up where the last programmer left off. But, you probably already know all this."

"I do," I admitted, "but on a much smaller scale than you."

"I understand. Well, not to scare you, but this WebCutter product is a behemoth of about one hundred million lines of code."

"One hundred million lines? You must be joking."

"No joke," he laughed, "and you'll get a chance to find out all about it. More than you'll ever want to know."

I grew excited at the thought. "When will I get a project?"

"Soon. I'm tying up loose ends on three other projects right now. As soon as I'm done I'll get you started on some bugs. But before that you need to start understanding Beamer WebCutter. I'm going to have you read some manuals." He searched his office. "If I can ever find the manuals."

Stacks of paper teetered in piles on his desk. He moved stack after stack aside. He checked several cabinets, he looked under a cluttered table, he opened boxes filled with technical manuals, and then he stood in the room thinking out loud with his hand over his mouth.

"Now where did I put those? Did someone borrow them? I thought they were on this desk, but...oh! Look at that. There they are sitting underneath this monitor. This damn monitor always seemed to sit too low so I used the manuals as scaffolding. How do you like that? Seek and ye shall find."

He passed the manuals to me. I grabbed at them so readily that I had to stifle the urge to start reading immediately.

Ted pointed at the wall, "You see these certificates here? These are all patents, Johnny. I'm not trying to brag, but these pieces of paper will help your career sail. Beamer loves internal inventions. If you take initiative in creating an algorithm or an idea, you'll be rewarded with royalties and promotion points. Heck, I still get checks every now and then from some of these, even one patent from fifteen years ago. And currently, a project that I am finishing up will give me another patent. Just keep that in mind. In twenty-two years, I've received ten patents."

I said, "Twenty-two years. Did it go fast?"

He paused for a thought. "Yes. Everything goes fast. Even at your age, you can look back at the speed of thought and see how fast high school and college went, right? But now that you brought it up, you've reminded me of my original plan when I first arrived here at your age. I only planned on doing one year of work here, then going back to school so I could teach math at Penn State. That was my original goal. But after that first year here, I decided to stay for the wages. At the time, I couldn't imagine going back to macaroni-and-cheese every night after I'd been exposed to a real diet, with money in my pocket. Know what I mean?"

I smiled, "Yes, my diet needs much improvement. You could still get your doctorate and teach college someday."

"Some days I still consider pursuing it, but I'm

comfortable here. I may regret it someday, but to take night classes alongside my work schedule would be downright crazy. Oh well, time marches on, as they say. I suppose if I hadn't done anything with my life, I might have regretted working all those Beamer nights and weekends, when I could have been golfing or on vacation instead."

We both laughed at free-will, or fate, whichever came first. My admiration for Ted increased with every word he spoke. He was a Beamer's Beamer that I aspired to emulate.

Ted wished me well, "Good luck on reading those manuals. They will fiercely bore you, no doubt. When you get bored, just take a walk. Also, Johnny, let me warn you: Sometimes it's hard to adjust to life at Beamer, so if you have any problems, come and talk to me, right?"

With a handshake I assured him that any problems I encountered would be brought to him. On the walk back to my office, the Beamer hallways baffled my sense of direction, much like the neighborhood streets where I lived with Jamie. After several minutes of wandering aimlessly, I found a map of Beamer posted on a wall, which cured my misdirection.

As soon as I walked back into my office, Danny said, "Listen to this, Johnny. 'Dow stocks dive one hundred points today. Shares of Microsoft lead the tumble.' That's no surprise, huh?"

Not knowing how to respond, I mumbled recognition, and opened one of the WebCutter manuals Ted had given to me. I am not ashamed to say that my toes curled in excitement as I read the introduction to the manual:

"Beamer WebCutter 6.0 is the centerpiece of your online business. No other software solution offers the same reliability, scalability, adaptability, or portability. Annually, Beamer

WebCutter leads the market in benchmarking and sales due to our architectural and technical edge. No other product is as technically sound or backed by such a dedicated Team."

Chills ascended and descended my spine. I continued to read until Danny interrupted me for the second time.

Danny read out loud, "Oh. My. God. Listen to this: 'Baseball stadium amendment proposed for state legislature.'"

"Mmmhmm," I mumbled.

"That is ridiculous. That amendment had better not pass, let me tell you. Taxpayers do not need to be paying for a billionaire's revenue problems. Give me a break."

"Mmmhmm." I continued to read the manual, but I'd gone no further than a paragraph when Danny read out loud yet another news item.

"'Minneapolis woman intends on opening a new orphanage to avoid making children bounce from foster home to foster home.'"

"Mmmhmm," I said, "Sounds like a noble idea."

Danny disagreed, "I think <u>she</u> should be put into a foster home. Just another bleeding heart in need of a neck tourniquet. Windbags. Listen to this, it goes on from here" ad nauseum.

Once again, I read the manual, but Danny continued to interrupt me every minute for the remainder of the day, ruining my concentration. At 4:00 in the afternoon, I collected my manuals and went home to read in peace.

On arriving home, I noticed a few mayflies flitting nearby the house, enjoying their one day of life. Each summer on the Mississippi river, mayflies emerge from the water and flutter around with sticky little bodies for one day of life, and in doing so irritate all of those people living near the river. When I stepped out of the car, a mayfly landed on my white shirt, to take a rest, then quickly flew away. He left a brown stain from his sticky body that outlined where he had perched on my shirt, but I smiled to think of his urgency to fulfill all of his little mayfly dreams in a matter of one day. As I approached the house, I noticed another mayfly sitting on a garage door panel, and he slowly separated his wings and closed them again.

"Shoo fly! Shoo!" I said, but he stayed put.

"Shoo fly! Shoo!" I said, but he ignored me.

I implored him, "Don't you want to enjoy the one day you've been allotted? Won't you fly about and mate with another pretty girl mayfly?" He opened his wings slowly and closed them again.

Suddenly the reality of his predicament dawned on me. He had landed on the garage door for a rest, but had settled too long in the rays of the sun. His comfort turned fatal as the gentle sunbeams warming him welded his sticky torso to the hot garage door. I remained with the little mayfly until he ceased his slow, dramatic opening and closing of wings. His yearning for comfort turned into his own sunny grave! Imagine the naïvety of a mayfly!

/* Encounters with a dog, a derelict, and the peaceful geese */

For the next three hours at home, I studied my manual with intense interest. Once the intensity faded, I resolved to take a stroll around my neighborhood in hopes of meeting a neighbor or two.

The hot summer sun was preparing for its daily nap. Shadows began to lurk from their hiding spots. The quiet of the neighborhood spread to all visible corners. I marveled at the serenity of my day. From my work, to my car, to my home, all was quiet (except for Danny and the whir). I peered down the street as far as possible to examine the neighborhood. Every house shared an almost identical motif, and everything appeared in order at each house, with both garage doors closed, lawns mowed, windows shut, and no toys in the yard. I walked to the end of my block, turned right, and ran into a brown squirrel on the sidewalk. In his paws he held an acorn that he sniffed and twirled. He completely ignored me as I stepped right over his bushy tail. In my short life experience, such trusting harmony between man and beast I'd never experienced.

I changed direction down a different street and spotted a man washing his automobile. He drove a fine car, so I accosted him to relay a compliment.

I said, "That's a fine vehicle you have there, sir."

The man said, "Thank you," then returned to washing his car.

I introduced myself and divulged the fact that I worked at Beamer.

The man said, "Is that right? I'm also a Beamer."

"You too?" I said with amazement. "What luck I have; the first person I approach in my new neighborhood works at the same place I do."

He said, "Actually, Johnny, the odds were pretty good. Many folks in this area work at Beamer."

"That's interesting," I said, "since it's so far from here to the Beamer site."

"People like to get away from work."

"I suppose it must be."

The man said, "Which house did you buy?"

"I'm renting one up the street," I said.

He looked at me sideways, "You shouldn't throw your money away on rent. Start building some equity right away."

"But, sir, I'm certainly not prepared for such a commitment yet."

"Suit yourself, but you're just throwing your money away. But, I guess you'll learn in time."

A woman emerged from the doorway with a dog drawn on a long leash. The dog instantly emitted a cylinder of poo on the lawn, prompting the woman to immediately bend over and scoop the glistening cylinder into a plastic bag. The dog then rolled on the grass playfully, which provoked an urgent response from the man.

"Get her off the lawn! It was sprayed today!"

The wife grew distraught on hearing this. "Where are the

signs? Didn't those Chemlawn idiots put up the little signs?" she asked.

"I took them down," said the man.

"Those men are apes anyway. I saw them last week; three of them joking around. They are like the drywallers that came here; three people for one little job."

The dog continued to scratch his back on the grass, completely carefree of chemical exposure. I said to the couple, "That dog reminds me of a dog I once owned that had no qualms with all things disgusting. He was always chewing on a placenta or fighting a rabid raccoons. Boy was he fun, may he rest in peace. One day I threw a stick too far and the poor thing drowned in a manure pit."

The woman's face contorted into a grotesque shape. She said nothing to me as she produced from her pocket two matching red-checkered bandanas. One bandana she tied around the neck of the dog and the other bandana she tied on her head.

She said to me, "Would you like to meet Hunter?"

"Is that his name?" I asked.

"Her. She's a boxer," the woman said.

"Well, hello dog!" I prattled, "Howdy-doo, dog! You must feel better after stooling on the grass, no?"

"She's a she. Her name is Hunter, not 'dog.'"

"Yes, indeed. Good pooch. Good muttley, muttley, muttley-fella. You're a lucky one to have someone dress you up to look nice, since your face is so flat. Almost looks like you ran into a brick wall. Did you run into a brick wall, muttley? But you're a nice ugly hound, aren't ya."

The wife yanked the animal away from my reach. She said to her husband, "I'll be back in an hour." The man said nothing, he only watched her leave. The dog ran away from the woman with great zeal, but the leash quickly jerked the zeal clean off the dog. However, the dog forgot, and once again ran forward only to achieve the same abrupt result.

The man said to me, "It was nice to meet you, Johnny. Stop by some time."

With that I continued down the sidewalk path, smiling at my fortune of meeting a neighbor so quickly. As I walked away I heard the man joke quietly,

"Yes, thank you Johnny-boy for letting the soap dry. Now I have to start washing this thing all over. Moron."

For a long while I continued walking, admiring the continuity of the yards and houses. The blades of grass were as stout as any grass I'd ever encountered. Each blade had the shape of a little Roman broadsword, so I began to daydream of little Roman Armies; an Army in every yard. Yes, little happy Armies that could not shed their swords, nor could they ever be stabbed by the neighboring Army. But I abandoned this daydream when I stumbled into a finely groomed neighborhood park.

The park contained a man-made pond in the center, which produced a healthy bucolic effect. For a minute I felt outside of the suburb entirely. A gaggle of geese paddled about in the middle of the pond. The sun's summer vibes still hung on the horizon, and of course this added to the scene beautifully. I focused on the geese in the distance. The serenity of the geese struck an altruistic chord in me; they looked like a cooperative specie on the pond, as they also do when flying in the classic V-formation. A quintessential community based on love and tranquility, in times of feast or famine, sharing everything between them. I heard their gentle, calling-song in the distance:

"Honk!" which I presumed meant: "Hello, friend."

"It is remarkable," I said out loud to the atmosphere, "how calm the water is with the geese sitting on it, with all of them appreciating one another's company, and with all of them so vociferously honking support to one another:"

"Hello, friend."   "Hello, friend."   "Hello, friend."

"Hello, friend."   "Hello, friend."   "Hello, friend."

"Hello, friend."

As my feet drew me closer to the water's edge, I noticed a commotion in the pond; the geese flapped about in a riotous enterprise. To satisfy my curiosity, I crept near the pond to discern the nature of the activity, and to my surprise and to the shame of the geese, I caught them in a wicked act of theft. A wounded goose held a large piece of bread in his bill, and the others attacked him. The wounded goose attempted to flee the many able-bodied geese. The message had changed from 'Hello, friend' to 'Gimme!'

The wounded goose cried out pathetically as the mob pulled out his already ragged feathers. The feathers floated in the pond, and in the end, after the healthy geese stripped the wounded goose of his bread, the gaggle swam away leaving the victim alone and hungry. The serenity I'd seen in the distance turned into ruthless calamity upon closer inspection. I assumed that this episode must have been an exception to the rule of geese. Normally geese would never hurt another for selfish reasons, would they?

Suddenly a noise startled me from behind. I did an about-face. Near the park dumpster something moved. With caution I watched the garbage container. Fear seized my nerves when I witnessed a man crawl out of the dumpster with a bucket filled with a foul booty of selected trash. I crouched low, so that the filthy derelict would not notice me or attack me; I had heard about their murderous ways on the TV news shows. A mother standing in the park collected her children and dialed someone on her cell phone. I myself considered notifying the police, but as I waited and watched, two squad cars arrived at the park. In the distance I saw the police officers detain the vermin after a bit of what seemed a necessary struggle, and as the bum was handcuffed, his bucket of trash vittles fell upside down to the ground.

/* How Jamie's preparation for a party perplexed me.
*/

Events happened one after the other, as they often do in life. That weekend, Jamie invited me to join him in attending a party. After the two full weeks of reading manuals, I readily agreed, and we prepared ourselves for an evening of eventfulness. As we changed our clothes, Jamie played music that celebrated his faith with lofty lyrics that filtered into every silence:

"It is good to wait patiently

Till rescue comes from the Lord.

It is good for a man, when young,

To bear a yoke..."

In the course of that Beamer night, it became evident that Jamie harbored certain misgivings about his job at Beamer as he made an outpouring to me of his grievances. I listened to his confession of complaints.

He lamented, "I'm feeling disgusted with the assignment my manager has given me...I mean, he's going to make me a system administrator, for goodness sake. I intend to be a software engineer, not an administrator. I'd rather do anything else - anything that requires even the slightest degree of engineering. It's just not right."

I offered him purgatory. I said, "Perhaps it's only temporary."

Jamie smacked his lips and plunged into a lengthy discourse of whining while we dressed for the party. As a sidebar, he agonized over the attire he would wear to the party.

doubled my efforts to study. Had I grown up outside of Minnesota, I might have asked the voluble duo of Fillmore and Danny to stifle their conversations, but the Minnesota-nice social culture instilled in me prevented such heretic effrontery.

more painful than receiving the actual bullet. Oh, how I hated pulling the trigger on them, watching their little bodies squirm in the tall grass with their eyes closed, as they cried out, "Mew, mew, mew! I'm sooo hungry!!" At first we shot them in the belly with a BB gun, thinking they might die immediately. Not so. Originally, we used an air-powered BB gun, which meant that you shot the first BB, then watched the baby squirm while you pumped the gun ten times before shooting again. And again. And again, until the baby perished. After a few years of watching them squirm under the torture of the BB gun, we went to the humanitarian .22 rifle. Then of course we learned to shoot them in the head rather than the belly so that the squirming ended quicker. Go for the head-shot. I also found that stepping on their heads with a heavy boot allowed for the least amount of pain in the kittens, but feeling the little skull crack under the boot cracked my heart as well. The .22 rifle worked most efficiently, especially when you had already dug a tiny pauper's grave for the corpses. In those situations, you had to pretend to be heartless, otherwise you had to watch them starve for the next six days. I quickly learned that crying only makes the rifle harder to aim. And you could always cry later on, after you'd tossed the dirt on the pile of bodies and planted the little square Roman crosses in the dirt with the names printed on the wood with a black magic marker, R.I.P. They were on their way out anyway, just like the rest of us, only quicker. Poor little wuss-pusses.

After I told Danny and Fillmore that story, they looked at me with blank faces, and said nothing, which in some ways was an accomplishment in itself. I assumed that they felt as sorry for the kittens as I did.

I returned to reading my manuals. But after so many distractions I found myself staring through the book into blurry Nevermore. Due to the level of distraction caused by Danny and Fillmore, I decided to start arriving at work earlier to reduce the hours I'd be subjected to cat and news stories. At home, I wouldn't believe. This cat is like no other. I was vacuuming and Mr. Pococurante was laying in the path of the vacuum. Mr. Pococurante absolutely refused to move out of the way. He absolutely refused to move, the lazy bum. So I just started pushing him around with the vacuum cleaner. He rolled along like a bowl of Jell-O. Finally, he got tired of being used as a mop, so he got up and sat on top of the vacuum cleaner while it was running, and he stayed there. He rode on top of the vacuum."

"Can you believe that, Johnny?" Danny asked.

I said, "I can't believe it. Cats sure are quirky. Perhaps he enjoyed the vacuum because of the warmth."

Fillmore whinnied, "Oh, who knows what goes on inside that cat's head! He's such a character. He is a great thespian, I tell you. I always catch him sitting in the window batting his paw at the Birds all day, never conceding the utter futility of the practice."

Danny supported Fillmore. "He does. I've seen it. He does, Johnny."

I gave in. I decided to share a story. The discussion of cats led me to tell Fillmore one of my childhood stories of kittens. I told her and Danny about the spring kittens. Kind of a sad story, or perhaps a happy story. It depends of course on one's philosophy toward existence. Every spring on the farm, a cat neglected her offspring until the kittens began to starve, and no orphanages or kindly nuns exist in the natural world. My sibling and I tried to feed the gaping little mouths, but trying to feed the kittens just made the inevitable death more painful for both parties, human and feline. Trying to feed the kittens took three to four hours a day and resulted in failure every spring we tried it. We soon realized that the .22 caliber rifle brought them to kitty heaven less painfully - more quickly. My sibling and I drew straws for executioner duty. Pulling the trigger may have been in the taller grass. Anyway, where was I?). Oh yes, so I opened the yard fence a few inches because I felt like pulling some weeds out of the flower beds. Before I could even turn around, that neighbor's dog came into our yard and terrorized Mr. Pococurante. The poor kitty nearly broke his little neck climbing a tree to escape the crazed animal."

Danny interjected, "I would tell the neighbor to lock the dog up or get a lawyer."

"Well," Fillmore huffed, "I went right to the neighbor and told him what happened and he apologized over and over. But still, that dog should have been on a leash. I am considering confronting the owner more formally about the incident, maybe with a formal letter so I have a paper trail documenting the dog's actions. I mean, for God's sake, the dog stayed in our yard for about fifteen minutes barking up the tree after Mr. Pococurante. Mr. Pococurante's fur was all puffed out. He was so scared. After the dog finally left our yard (once I scolded the neighbor), poor Mr. Pococurante wouldn't come down from the tree. The poor kitty; he was terrified. I nearly called 911."

Still I read onward, holding my tongue in favor of my attempt at diligence. I read,

"In this environment, working with such NULL characters will produce a system fault."

But Fillmore went on with the cat story. There was always more to it. "But then after Mr. Pococurante finally came out of the tree, Mr. Pococurante did the cutest thing once he came back in the house. Oh my God, Danny. He did that thing with the vacuum again."

Danny said, "Johnny, you have to meet Fillmore's cat sometime. He is something else."

Fillmore went on, "Oh yeah, he has personality like you

mell sort, as follows:

I would read a bit of manual, such as something riveting like, *"Weak references allow a program to maintain a reference to an object that does not prevent the object from being considered for reclamation by the garbage collector."*

And Danny would kindly share an opinion about an odd topic, such as, "I don't care what anyone says; there wouldn't be laws against men dating little girls if it wasn't a fact that men want to date little girls. That's the way many men think. I'm not saying anything about myself, that's just the way it is."

I read another page, but spent twenty minutes processing it due to the distractions, *"In general a thread synchronizes itself with another thread by 'putting itself to sleep.' When the thread sleeps, the operating system no longer schedules CPU time for the thread, and the thread therefore stops executing. Just before the thread begins sleeping, however, the thread tells the operating system what 'special event' (such as a keystroke, mouse click, and algorithm completion) must occur for the thread to start executing again."*

While Danny scoffed, "Listen to this one, just off the wire: 'Microsoft admits security hole in online e-mail accounts.' Like that's a surprise. Oh my God!"

And Fillmore's cat, without exception, had a story that merited a long discussion, such as, "Yesterday the neighbor's dog came after Mr. Pococurante. Oh, it still makes me mad to think about. I was so upset. Little Mr. Pococurante was out playing in *our* yard (which is fenced in, Johnny, in case you didn't know). Mr. Pococurante was minding his own business, kind of rolling around in the grass (which is really adorable by the way. We must have some natural catnip or aromatic plant that he likes in our yard. Sometimes I wait to mow in the backyard just for that reason; so Mr. Pococurante can roll around

I asked, "What kind of party have you been invited to, Jamie?"

He said, "It's just an informal gathering that's been arranged by an acquaintance of mine. Also, Johnny, I forgot to mention: there is a fellow I met online that will be stopping over who needs a ride to the party. I offered our services to him."

"What a socialite you are, Jamie. I haven't met anyone yet in the city. It will be nice to have a visitor here."

"Won't it, though?" he smiled.

"It will."

Shirt after shirt donned Jamie's frail torso as he desperately searched for the perfect party ensemble. His selection of eyewear troubled him even more than his choice of shirt, as he first decided to remove his contact lenses in favor of glasses, but after deliberation and discombobulating, he put the contact lenses back in, which required him to again comb his hair in order to remove a crease created by the glasses, and to comb his hair he decided to douse his head with water and start the whole procedure from the beginning. While this all occurred I sat on the couch holding a brown bottle of pilsner.

The doorbell announced the arrival of our guest, so I opened the front door. Hearing the doorbell, Jamie swiftly strode across the living room to shake the hand of the gentleman who stood in the doorway.

"You must be Juan," Jamie said.

"I am."

I said, "Would you care to partake of a beverage, Juan?"

Juan at first stood still, causing Jamie and I to listen with rapt attention for his answer. No one moved an inch as Juan pondered the question. As for myself, I felt it incumbent upon me to convey my welcome to Juan by tilting my head and offering a smile in his direction. Jamie did the same. We leaned forward. Leaning. Leaning. When both Jamie and I leaned as far forward on our toes as we could manage without falling, Juan said,

> "I…" said Juan.
>
> We leaned closer…
>
> "…will have a…"
>
> Leaning closer…
>
> "I will have a beer," said Juan.

"Phew!" the whole room exhaled anxiety. Then, unexpectedly, Jamie said, "I, too, will have a beer."

I imparted an inquisitive look to Jamie, to remind him of his temperance in case he had forgotten his abstinence for an instant. On seeing my questioning face, Jamie nodded his head vigorously in confirmation of his beer request.

* * * * *

The three of us discussed our jobs in the graceful music. I told the story of my attempts to read manuals amid the hubbub caused by Fillmore and Danny, which made both Jamie and Juan laugh.

Juan admitted that he, too, worked in the booming information technology industry, only he worked at a hospital instead of Beamer. Juan explained his position in life. "I've hit a ceiling," he said, "or maybe a plateau, but whatever it is, I can see little mobility for my future at the hospital" mobility meaning money. "The websites I design are two years behind in terms of new technologies. The hospital chooses to allocate as little money as possible for my department; meaning new systems and software rarely get purchased. I don't know what I'll end up doing, but I need to increase my skill set."

Jamie said, "Perhaps you might consider pursuing an MBA?"

"Yes, I've considered it, but I prefer to stay in the web design field. I desire to work in a place that encourages research and experimentation. Something creative. The changes going on in this field right now happen at such a blazing and phenomenal pace that to be idle at all invites a moss of mediocrity to gather. Also, by the time I decide on learning a new technology, another technology spawns from the primordial internet ooze to add to my confusion. Plus, in my job, where we wait until the technology is obsolete, I spend the majority of my day updating mundane crap on the web site or doing data entry. There are just too many changes occurring to keep up with."

I said, "It's true. I believe that people like us would be wise to select one or two areas to become experts in, because to attempt studying every new technology that entered the marketplace would consume all of our time."

Juan said, "There's not enough time in a day."

"Never."

"Not ever."

We agreed on these points redundantly. Juan asked Jamie about the status of his job at Beamer, and Jamie produced a new version of his opinion that contradicted all of his earlier negativity.

Jamie said, "Well, I am very happy to be a Beamer and will soon be a systems administrator. My manager wants me to fill a role in the department that is lacking, so I find that it's a great opportunity for me to learn that segment of the business. I'd like to get into engineering within a few years, God willing. Either way, my manager and I have mapped out a tentative five-year career plan that I am very excited about."

Based on Jamie's earlier *petit mal* over his job, my face turned to bewilderment. I asked Jamie, "I thought you hated the idea of system administration. Is that not so anymore?"

Jamie blushed, "Did I lead you to that impression? Sorry, Johnny. I apologize for speaking unclearly. Of course, it is true; I want to be a programmer as well, but I'm just taking my career one stepping stone at a time." Jamie smiled at me and nodded, but I could only offer him a vacant stare. My empty bottle of beer indicated that the conversation had ended.

I said, "Bottoms up now, eh? Shall we leave for the party? I have nothing against either of you, but I am looking forward to meeting a beautiful woman this evening. Don't you guys agree?"

And neither of them responded, so I felt silly, and looked at the ground. But the pious songs of Jesus went on faithfully in the background:

"My words have been frivolous: what can I reply?

I had better lay a hand over my mouth.

I have spoken once, I shall not speak again,

I have spoken twice; I have nothing more to say."

/* How I met you, Katya, at the party. */

Katya, you know the story of this night as well as I, but I enjoy replaying the moments that I spent with you. Particularly this memory, because it was the first time I met you. Also, dear Katya, I apologize in advance for offensive commentaries, but reality's vinegar cannot be forever drowned by sugar.

It came to pass that the three of us arrived late for the party, bringing to Jamie a sensation of truancy and irresponsibility. Until the moment we reached the door, he expressed concerns over whether or not he'd perhaps missed any of the revelry within the house. Using my best effort, I assured him that 9:00 in the evening was entirely too early to have missed anything overly undomesticated.

I said to Jamie, "Don't be nervous. You're an acquaintance of one of the people here, right?"

Jamie said, "Actually I don't know anyone here. I just know the party is open to anyone who wants to attend."

I said, "Well, don't be nervous or you'll make me nervous."

Juan said, "And me nervous, too."

When we entered the door an attractive, blonde woman greeted us and escorted us into the living room. Immediately inside my thoughts I thanked Jamie for leading me to a house of such comeliness, but upon rounding the corner and perusing the faces of the other guests, I retracted my inner thanks, as only our blonde hostess and one brunette attracted my overall sensory.

The hostess asked the three of us what we preferred to drink, and I unwittingly said, "Beer" although no one in the living room appeared to have anything but soda.

Jamie whispered, "Johnny, I don't think they have any beer."

Our blonde hostess smiled, "Yes, we do have some. It's just that hardly anyone has requested it."

Juan sheepishly said, "Then, may I also have a beer?"

And Jamie returned to his abstinence, saying, "I will have a soda."

I followed our hostess to the kitchen to help her transport the drinks, and this allowed a window of opportunity for familiarization. In following her, I noticed her long, straight, blonde hair reached the small of her back stopping approximately one inch above her compact waistline, and it also occurred to me that the distance from her waistline to her toes, down the curvaceous seam of her taut, black pants, possibly exceeded a full five feet of leg. I exaggerate. But the length of her body did summon my mouth into a garrulous mood.

I joked, "Should I call you 'hostess,' or how may I address you?"

She laughed, "Oh, goodness, I'm sorry! How rude of me. I'm Libby."

I lavished a reply to her. Libby's mischievous pants hung pleasantly on her hipbones as she bent down to the refrigerator, and in bending, an angle of light exposed the contents of her shirt unto me. I averted my eyes as propriety would have it, but soon succumbed once again to enjoy the revelation. She handed the beverages to me one at a time, which movement bounced the exposed contents of her shirt in a jocular, circular pattern.

Feeling compelled to speak as I took in Libby's breasts, I said, "Is this your house?"

Libby said, "No, actually I rent from one of the guys in the living room. He's the one playing the guitar."

"Oh, ok," I said, "so is this a regular group of people that commune together?"

She stood erect and closed off my mammary line of sight. "Yes it is a regular get-together. We get together quite often for casual evenings."

"Casual evenings, yes. That sounds perfect after a long week of Beamer nights."

She brightened, "Oh, you work at Beamer?"

"I do."

"That's great."

"Yes, it is," I said.

She asked, "So what do you do at Beamer?"

"I'm a software engineer."

"That is so awesome," she smiled.

"Well, it certainly was not a cool thing to be in college."

"No? Well, it should be. Lots of money in that field. So I'm told," she laughed.

"Yes, I've heard that, too. And what do you do, Libby?"

"I'm a child care coordinator."

"Oh yeah?"

"Yes. It's *great*. It's really a great job. You know I spend most of my days with kids, so how can anyone complain about that?" She and I gushed a snort of giggles at the remark.

I continued, "And what else do you do for pleasure and enjoyment in this world?"

She brushed her hair out of her face and said, "Movies, books," then she pointed toward the ceiling and said, "I spend most of my time getting closer to Him."

I looked upward, "To whom?"

She pointed to the ceiling again, "Him."

Confused, I asked, "Does someone live upstairs?"

"No, silly!" She folded her arms. "I mean God, of course!"

At that moment a song began to emanate from the living room mariachi, and a realization sponged over me...

"Are you close to God?" Libby asked.

I squinted my eyes. "Yes, I believe so," I reasoned, "If man is the image of God, of course, then yes, for sure, maybe."

She nodded at me and slowly responded. "That's a good answer. I like that...I like that. You should attend our study group on Wednesday. We meet once a week and select a few readings from the Bible to study. This week we are reading Paul's letter to Titus."

"Paul...Titus, yes."

"Yes, you should come." She touched my arm.

"I would like to. Perhaps I should get closer to God," meaning closer to Libby.

"Absolutely. Everyone should."

With that Libby and I moved back into the living room with the others. Jamie appeared more relaxed as the guitar played soothing Jesus songs that I knew Jamie enjoyed. I approached Jamie and interrupted his listening.

I whispered, "Psst, Jamie - I think you picked out a Christian party for us to go to."

He whispered, "Yes, I know that."

I said, "But you didn't tell me. I had no idea."

Jamie paused and looked at me. "I know. I'm sorry for not telling you. I thought you might enjoy it."

Relieved, I said, "Oh!...well, thank you for considering me. I've already enjoyed an oblique aspect of our hostess, whose name is Libby..."

Jamie snapped, "Shhh, now! I want to listen."

The song ended and the people in the living room ejaculated into a round of clapping. The man holding the guitar then spoke as one with authority, exhorting thanks to those of us newcomers at the party.

"Here we are all bondservants to Christ Jesus," the guitar player said while strumming through a sad set of minor chords, "And everyone is welcome here. We want you all to feel comfortable, as this evening is a party of observance for the one true religion, in the name of our Savior, Jesus Christ, who loved and tolerated everyone for all the days of His life, and died for our sins so that we might reach heaven by accepting Him and everyone on earth into our pitiful hearts."

I tipped my bottle to a high angle and swallowed; 'cheers' to Jesus! I felt a sense of spirit filling me. Libby then started singing a new song unto the room. I ducked into the kitchen and pilfered two beer bottles from the refrigerator. With a skilled rapidity I emptied both bottles into my stomach cavity before I returned to the living room with a third bottle in hand. The room roared with applause as Libby finished the song in full and unrestrained vibrato, which shook her cleaved bosom nicely,

"Cause I'm just like Lazaru-u-u-u-u-s..."<raucous applause>

I held my beer in one hand and clapped along with the other; I hooted appreciation of the singing beauty and praised the creation of God Almighty.

Across the room the only other attractive woman, the brunette, rolled her eyes at Libby's rendition of the song. For the next thirty minutes songs were sung, praises were offered to ancient men, and my thirst directed me to the refrigerator repeatedly as I reached a higher state of mind. At the end of each performance, I returned to the living room to issue my own clapping and whistling; I must say, the warm spirit of the Paraclete enveloped me wholly.

At the end of one song, I said in boisterous prayer, unsure of how to pray, "For the love of all things uncertain! - Praise be to what is and what never will be!"

The brunette, who had beautiful dark features, increased her scowl as time passed. I became concerned and watched her disapproval increase with each song; I wished to subtly catch her attention to initiate a discussion about the root of her displeasure. Suddenly, in the middle of a song about an amazing reactionary named Saul of Tarsus, the brunette rose from her seat and walked swiftly in the direction of the kitchen. I followed her to see if I could diagnose her scowl, and perhaps prescribe a remedy of some kind. She was clearly not receiving into her heart the same spirit that I was. In the kitchen, before I said anything to her, I swerved clumsily into a tall planter and knocked dirt all over the floor, then I followed up the performance with spilling beer on the spilled dirt, then breached the second commandment with swearing, which the brunette found quite humorous. Hearing her laugh inspired me to pathetically choke the plant as if it had accosted me in the first place.

I choked the stem of the plant, saying, "What's the matter with you plant? Who put you there? Answer me! I want the truth!"

And on the brunette's winsome face where the scowl had drooped a smile was born. With my best attempt at gentility, I introduced myself and asked her name, and she said in a sweet voice that sounded better than any song,

"Katya."

***

Oh Katya! Do you remember it all as clearly as I do? You were such a lady, with such a dark and pure countenance...you were altogether blossoming!

/* What went on in the kitchen regarding Katya's displeasure leading to my pleasure. */

Inasmuch as your hand, Kayta, rested on the refrigerator door unoccupied, I joined my hand upon yours until you discontinued the union. You laughed at my ridiculous method of taking your hand.

"Katya," I said, "if I might pry into your mood, you seem irritated by the singing in the living room. Is this true or am I being too nosy?"

"That is very accurate, in fact. A friend of mine from work invited me to this party without telling me what the agenda was."

"Agenda?" I asked with confusion. "Do you mean the order of songs?"

"No. I mean the atmosphere of the party."

"Too humid?"

"No."

"Too dry?"

"Not at all."

"You have allergies then?"

"No. It is the level of abstract horseshit."

"Horseshit!" I exclaimed far too loudly.

You smiled at my outburst, and poured a glass of wine.

I whispered, "Horseshit? What do you mean? Literal or figurative horseshit? Am I to believe that you find these people similar to barnyard animals?"

"Only when they throw recruitment parties that I'm duped into attending."

"What a thing to say!" I said, "I'm not being recruited; my roommate invited me. How can you allege such an accusation at God-loving people?"

You said, "Well, were you briefed on what type of party this would be?"

I said, "In fact, I was not, but I believe Jamie merely forgot. He's quite forgetful tonight."

You shook your head and said with a knowing voice, "This is a detail one does not forget."

"Katya, are you telling me that you have not chosen Christ as your savior, and in doing so have shunned yourself out of Heaven and instead into the terror, the pit, and the snare of everlasting damnation?"

"That's right, I have. Start mourning for me now, Johnny. I have not accepted this religion, just as I have not accepted the Hindu, Islamic, Orthodox, Zoroastrian, Buddhist, Aristotelian, Wiccan, Stoic, Bokonon, or any other figment of mankind's imagination that attempts to declare truth of the unknown."

"What a list of words!" I whispered with exclamation. "And none of these suit you, Katya? Perhaps you might find a religion you enjoy yet?"

"You mean another philosophy or theology?" you asked.

"Yes, I suppose."

You laughed, "If I hear one more naked theoretician or convinced theologian explain the unexplainable, it will be too much for me. But that's enough of this, Johnny, I can see you should not be at this place either; you are too ready to swallow. Let's drink."

I complied with your plan, Katya. Before long, you and I grew rather rowdy in the kitchen as we exchanged jokes and stories. During one of my stories I swung my arm and knocked a bottle to the floor where it shattered in a loud fuss, which startled the guests in the living room. The singers and audience stopped singing and clapping. The party members made their way toward the kitchen in search of this newfound sound of celebration, but when you heard the voices of Jamie and the other worshippers coming around the corner, you threw your arms around my neck and whispered in my ear,

"Johnny, kiss me, now!"

And I complied, with feelings of great joy. Your mouth met mine; you stung my heart. Our hands drifted all over, much to the pleasure of my outer regions. And when Libby and the guitarist and Jamie and Juan and the rest of the party entered the kitchen, they stopped moving and they all sinned in unison:

"Oh my GOD!"

Now midway out the door of the house, Katya, you charged me with the duty of driving, so I decided to call a cab on my cell phone. The guitar player shouted out loud, saying that you and I were banished from his house forever, and his excommunication of you provoked a great tirade from you, Katya. How fired up you became, Katya - expressing your detestation for fanatic enlistment parties, citing many examples of similar events that I had previously been unaware of. The door tersely slammed behind us as we stepped outside, and as we moved away from the door the voices in the house grew invigorated.

At this point I had fallen in love with you, Katya.

Outside, east of Eden, to kill time we smoked cigarettes and tossed the spent butts on the lush green lawn. Occasionally heads dandled in the windows of the house as the Christians peered out to determine if we had yet departed to Gomorrah or had been struck dead by lightning. Jamie's head appeared in the window, shaking from side to side, with his jaw moving up and down, and his forehead crinkled into horizontal shelves. I waved to him, but he apparently failed to see me because he did not return the gesture. I remember, Katya, how you watched the heads appear in the windows and laughed.

"Thank you, Johnny," you said, "It is right to give them opportunities to expose their hypocrisies. The best people at judging and excluding others are those that claim to never judge anyone. That's why I kissed you, in case you were wondering."

I said, "Katya, may I say with all honesty that your kisses are amazing."

You then assured me that my reception of the affection was spur of the moment only, a means to an end, and that I should not blindly expect any encores.

I needled you by saying, "Thy will be done, Katya."

You laughed, "Oh, you're a funny one, Johnny."

O my Katya! You laughed so lovely, and then you did kiss me again, mostly to irritate those in the house, but I imagined the affection to be generated from desire.

During the kiss, I peeked at the house and witnessed the whole congregation standing in the window horrified with gaping maws.

/* How I somehow managed to start a fight at a nightclub and thus met the drywallers three. */

In this portion of the account, I'd prefer to not address you directly, Katya. I feel that doing so makes me seem desperate for you, which of course, I am. Desperation is not only the English way; it is also the Pepper family way. And though I'm sure you remember the following events as well as I do, I want to record the night in its entirety, so that a record exists of the significant Beamer nights for posterity. So if you prefer, you can skip this part about my unfortunate ignorance of how to act in a nightclub. The following chapter may be of more interest to you.

* * * * *

Katya and I stood outside until the cab arrived and whisked us to a Minneapolis nightclub known as *The Aviary*. Right away, Katya ordered drinks and I began observing the people attending the club. I felt quite virgin to this venue, to be sure. Katya returned with two glasses and plopped an elfin drink in front of me.

She said, "You owe me eight dollars."

"Eight dollars?" I said with surprise.

"Yes, eight."

I mused, "The drinks must be excellent here, seeing how little the glasses are and how great the cost."

Katya said, "This place is excessive in all ways - I seldom come here for that reason, but sometimes a girl has to go out among the worldlings we share the planet with, for laughs if nothing else. The Aviary is like any other nightclub, meaning it is full of bullies, conspicuous consumption, ostentatious displays, and of course, the staple of exclusionary pastimes, superficial beauty. But tonight, after attending that sanctimonious party, I feel the need to get out. I need to be around some actual human beings, of which this place is in great surplus, for better or for worse. I think I'd like to dance for a while. You may join me, or hang out here, or leave, or choose any other fate for this evening. Whatever is fine with me."

With those choices, I opted to stay seated for a spell in order to observe the multimedia display of people, lights, and sounds. Katya plunged into the flocks of people in the dancing pond, disappearing in an instant from my sight. The nightclub had a bounty of activity going on in every corner, perch, and knothole. The entire audience in the center moved in a unified frenzy. A few females found themselves on a platform wriggling furiously to the sound in order to attract male members of the audience, and success came to those females time and again as large breasted males clawed their way through the crowd to reach the platform; the crowd was strictly survival-of-the-amorous in this respect. Females of colorful plumage walked past where I sat, and even though I loved Katya already, my eyes and inner thoughts noticed each set of thin, shiny legs. I am a simple man.

Distinct groups of males in close formations moved around the perimeter of the nightclub in search of something, though I had no idea what, and at the front of each group stood one male who appeared to be in charge of the flock behind him. Likewise, assemblages of females bunched together at tables, looked around furtively, and engaged each other in energetic chatter. Some individuals strutted around by themselves, most of whom wore highly unique attire and accoutrements, such as the one male I noticed with sharp quills protruding from his face, and the female who painted one shock of her hair with pink dye and another portion with blue dye. I did not intend to directly interact with the bionetwork in front of me, but Fortune had decided otherwise.

I sipped slowly on my tiny saucer of drink when unexpectedly a white male with large biceps confined in his very small jet-blue t-shirt approached me with a question.

He said, "What are you lookin' at, rubberneck?"

Unsure of what to specifically answer, I shrugged and said, "Everything."

His face tightened like a fist. "I think your eyes wander too much."

I said, "Not at all. I think this whole place is fabulous."

His faced adorned a look of incredulity. "Fabulous?" he said and smirked at his gathering friends. "You think this place is fabulous? What are you, a flamer or something?"

In my ignorance I informed him that I was, in fact, a 'flamer,' supposing that the word might be a gang thing or win myself some kind of approval. I judged incorrectly. He immediately deduced that I intended to mock him, and he said he was watching me stare at the female he'd tagged as his own, and he declared my looking around to be offensive, and he generously offered me a proposition where I might find my own mother downtown somewhere that very night if I had two dollars to spend, which was preposterous since she had died when I was a very little boy. I spent a minute or two assuring the fellow that he should not feel ashamed or bitter about me looking at his female because I had watched every female that walked past, and of all the females I saw, I looked at his particular female the least due to the abundance of those that I found more appealing.

But after this response he liked me even less. He so

despised me that he emptied my saucer of eight-dollar liquor onto my head and enthusiastically begged me to hit him in the face, but I declined, expecting that he would then want to hit me back. His chest puffed outward to a great extent. Several of his white male friends closed in on his flanks, and they too wore tight jet-blue t-shirts. This additional support caused my aggressor's chest to grow ever more inflated. The males on his flanks grew highly agitated, and they flapped their arms more and more as the man urged me to strike him. I continued to sit silently, dripping in booze, entirely unsure of what action to take. Without reason, I decided to stand up, and that's when he placed his beak right on my beak. The scene might have made a wonderful painting.

Suddenly I heard a loud squawking sound, as a group of females gathered around the standoff to share their viewpoints on the happenstance I'd involved myself in. The females urged various opinions, some wishing for me to be seated, some wishing for me to flail my fist at the man, and others stayed on the fence to scorn the whole situation. Just when I started to believe that my best plan of action was indeed to hit the male, a new set of voices twittered behind me.

I heard a raspy grackle of a voice say, "Go home. Haven't you learned yet that you are just a hopeless gangster wannabe?"

I imagined myself to be the intended listener, until my puffed-up aggressor responded to the raspy voice by saying, "Nice to see the trash made it out tonight. I thought the garbage was picked up on Thursday."

The voice behind me answered, "I've been watching this whole event unfold, and you are a punk-bully and nothing more."

Another voice behind me said, "Yes, and if you will not

sit down, we will find a chair to put you in."

A third voice, more garbled, said, "And also a schair for each of your vishous palss."

Hearing these new voices gave everyone involved a spirited boost: the females became cacophonous, the males rowdy, and my aggressor felt it necessary at this point to spit saliva directly into my left eyeball. With this development, I decided to accept his offer to hit him, but before I could even ball up a fist, one of the bodies from behind me sprung into view and savagely deflated the chest of my aggressor. With the fists flying in front of me, I stood in the midst dumbfounded, not knowing how to react at all, or least of all who to punch at. Soon the two other men behind me appeared in front of me and scattered all observers away from the squabble taking place on the floor. I wiped the spit off my face using my shirt sleeve. A swarm of fury cascaded through The Aviary, and captured the attention of everyone present, including the largest males of all, the bouncers, who swiftly dove in and separated the fools grappling on the floor. A bouncer escorted my blue-shirted antagonist out of the nightclub and sailed him into the night horizontally. My defenders exchanged many graphic metaphors with the antagonist's friends, and blue shirted troops eventually migrated back to their original territory, allowing me to feel relaxed once again. The three men who helped fend off my attacker expressed apologies for involving themselves in the predicament.

In disbelief, I said to them, "Are you guys kidding? Without your intervention I might have been killed. You see, I am a stripling software engineer at Beamer, not at all prone to such fight or flight situations. I don't know of any algorithm for this type of situation."

The man who fought in my defense, a latino man, said, "That man in your face is a frequent problem here. You were his prey for the evening. He gets mad every week."

The second man, a black man, said, "But he is still young. He'll adjust the hard way, I imagine. Maturing is a complex process for everyone."

The third man, a white man, slurred his foul words, saying, "Don't shugarcoat it; he's piece a' shee-it."

I offered to buy them all a drink. The latino said, "We'll take a drink. Especially from a rich man like yourself."

I said, "Oh, I'm not rich."

The black man said, "Even so, you will be someday."

I replied, "Yes, I hope to be someday maybe. But I would also like to experience a full life."

The white man said, "Well, a fisht full of green will shure help. And shonsh of bish-ez like us a picnic short," at which they all laughed, and I laughed along.

I asked them, "What do you guys do?"

"We are drywallers."

I said, "That's hard work."

The first man said, "It can be. When we have work to do. Our bosses get paid year round, whether or not there is work to do. But those who call the shots in businesses...man, they are never the ones in the line of fire."

The second man argued, "We have been without work for some time due to union and economic concerns. So when my partner and colleague here talks about the line of fire, he speaks too glibly. What he fails to realize is that, in reality, our bosses, or those who call the shots in general - they are always the ones in the line of fire. Without them we might be working warehouse jobs."

I listened and felt moved by the drywaller's discussion. I said, "It seems a lot of discussion is spent by people on that exact topic. Who calls the shots and who should earn what."

And the third man ended the topic, saying, "Shpeaking of shots, lets order some. Line up the shots, boys!"

The first drywaller said, "This drunkard here - his back is shot, and so is his liver and brain."

At that moment a tooth fell onto the table. It had fallen right out of the third drywaller's mouth, and the rest of us looked up at him in surprise. The third drywaller batted his tooth off the table and said, "Ffack 'em! Who needs 'em?" It seemed very strange to talk about a tooth that way.

Katya returned, freshly dampened from the ardor of the dance floor, with her long dark hair softly shining, looking lovely as a foxglove bell after light rain. Seemingly her petals asked for me to touch them in the winking lights, but before I could say anything flattering, the drywallers introduced themselves to Katya.

"Would you care to sit down?"

"Buy you a drink?"

"Ho-ho! Shlow down. Turn around and sh-show it to papa, you shweet dolly *llama*!"

Katya said, "Johnny, have you made some friends?"

The first drywaller said, "You missed the ruckus? Did you not see the events? Johnny fended off a rabid ostrich from attacking us."

The second drywaller said, "It's the truth.."

And the third said, "Who's thish luttle raggamuffin? I'm Jeff. Howdy-ooo. Can I get you anythphing? A place to shtay fffor the night?"

Katya said, "Are you sure it was this Johnny here that fended off an attacker?"

The first drywaller said, "It was."

The second, "We saw it."

And the third, "How's m'bout a ph-phone number? Gimme a ballpark figure. Or just the last four digits, maybe. Go ahead, whisper it to me, will ya?"

Katya said, "Sorry pal. Johnny is my date for the night. Rebel that he is."

My heart fluttered on hearing Katya say so.

The drywallers, Katya, and I went to an apartment, where we all engaged in long conversations. They were keenly aware of things I had no idea about, such as how to roll my own cigarettes using exotic, green tobacco, as well as various West Indian philosophies I had not heard of. We discussed all things Bokonon and I was quite taken in. Katya refrained from the smoke while I inhaled deep enough that the walls of the room appeared to grow flexing tentacles.

Later in the night, Katya kissed me once, twice, three times more, and handed me a folded piece of paper with her phone number written on it. The drunken drywaller, named Jeff, observed the exchange and slyly approached Katya and kissed her on the cheek. Then he kissed *me* on the cheek and grabbed my hand and wrote his phone number with a blue permanent marker on my skin. He said that I should call him some night for happy hour. I rewrote his number on a piece of paper and tucked it away in my wallet.

Katya and I stood near a concrete staircase that led to the basement. Jeff in his drunken state wobbled toward us one last time, then leaned backward and fell down the stairwell, tumbling backward and striking his head numerous times on various cement steps and the wood-paneled wall. Katya and I rushed down the stairs after Jeff the drywaller, worried that a serious trauma may have occurred. By the time we reached Jeff, blood had gathered on the crown of his head, enough to matt his hair down. The other two drywallers came down the stairs to look at Jeff, concerned for him in their own way.

Katya said to the coherent drywallers, "Where's Jeff's car? I can take him to the hospital."

One of the other drywallers said, "He can't go to the hospital."

Katya said, "What? Are you crazy? He could have a head injury."

The same drywaller said, "He doesn't have health insurance."

"So what," I stammered, "they'll take care of him at the hospital. That's their job!"

A drywaller said, "Yeah, it sure is. They will take care of him for about ten thousand dollars. Just stop the bleeding. Jeff will be fine in the morning."

Katya went to a phone on the wall and started to dial 911, but one of the drywallers took the phone out of Katya's hand and placed it back on the wall.

"Believe me, Katya. If tomorrow Jeff is not well, we will

take him to see someone. But if we were to take him to the hospital tonight, and he received a bill, he would be forced to use all of his saved money for the bill, and then he would not be able to pay child support for his daughter, who is the most important person in his life. He sends all the money that he doesn't drink away to his ex-wife for his little girl."

Jeff mumbled a few broken words from the floor. "Don't take me...to no...fffrickin' doctor...please...jus' leave me here."

Katya and I looked at each other and gave up trying to persuade the drywallers three. The conscious drywallers assured us they would keep watch over Jeff throughout the night. They told us to go home.

Katya and I took a cab back to my house where we entered the doorway as quietly as possible, but my decreased motor skills caused me to stumble into Katya and knock us both to the floor in a forceful crash. We regained our feet, ran down the hallway to my bedroom, and inside the room we burst out laughing. I kissed her with high hopes, but she said,

"Just go to sleep, Johnny."

Reluctantly I slept, but we did wake up later for a delightful, mutual recreation of playing busydigits and doodle-rub. Then we returned to sleep, and I believe that my eyes twinkled all night long, even after my lids set themselves down for rest.

/* What events occurred upon waking to find Katya gone. */

I awoke half past the afternoon and stretched my arms to my sides expecting to have an arm run into a sleeping Katya, but the meeting never took place. She had departed my room without waking me. I grew anxious as I searched the house, disturbed by the notion that I may have committed an irreparable act of indecency that coerced her exit, or that the entire occasion had been a dream of mine. Her absence put me in a worrisome state, as I am prone to fretting and anxiety, and I scorned myself for whatever I might have done. Oh, how I hated that action that I did not remember, or the lost act that might or might not have scared away the lovely Katya from my bedroom.

The anxiety hula-danced in my bowels and caused me to swiftly walk to the bathroom. But when I turned on the bathroom light, in the midst of scorning myself, I read a message written in lipstick on the bathroom mirror that said:

"Katya was here."

What relief; what joy in me bounced! And bounce it did - in direct opposition to the guilt and worry, causing a rapid requirement for me to be seated on the porcelain stool.

Later on, Jamie sat at his computer desk ignoring me. I sat down at my computer desk that faced his. He still did not acknowledge my presence.

I said, "Did your party go well, Jamie?"

Jamie said, "I'm not speaking to you."

"Why not?" I asked.

"Because of what you did at the party. I was fortunate to be accepted into the group after that obscenity."

"But I am sure that Katya may have taught them a fine lesson, too."

Jamie grew irritated, in no small degree. His eyes blazed. He said, "What lesson? Absolutely not."

"But is it true that, perhaps, you invited me only that I might be recruited to be more holy?"

Jamie scoffed, "Not at all."

I said, "But it is strange you would not mention where you were taking me."

"Well, it slipped my mind...and besides, you had no trouble finding your own party with that...woman."

"Do you mean Katya?"

"YES! That...*slut*."

Oh dear, oh dear. My knuckles instantly turned into twisted bundles in my lap as I stifled an awful urge to rebut Jamie bodily, but I remained calm in my voice.

I said, "Jamie, you should say you are sorry now. You have passed a horrible judgment on a person of whom you know nothing of, and you have dangerously upset my delicate balance within that has already run a gauntlet of emotions this morning (or this afternoon, rather). I finally met someone that I really like."

Jamie listened and slowly agreed. "Okay...I'm sorry. I don't want to ruin our friendship. But I wish to make it known that I will not tolerate late night noises from you or your guests, as happened last night."

I disagreed, "But surely you understand fun nights spent at parties may happen from time to time."

"I'd rather they did not. I have church on Sundays."

"But we must allow them, or else our rapport will quickly become unmanageable. Jamie, you see - I am fond of eventful living. Weakness is my strength; it has built my character."

Jamie shook his head and entered theology, "Yes, well perhaps you should try to change your weakness into something more. Perhaps you could attend church with me next week."

"Yesterday I would have agreed with you, but today I'd rather subscribe to Katya's viewpoints."

Jamie continued, "Then you are limiting yourself."

"On the contrary, I get more sleep on Sundays..."

Jamie said, "That is not how God sees it."

Feeling catty, I responded, "You've spoken?"

"God sees you as a lost child," Jamie said.

"Katya told me that God is in the bees, the milkweed, the caterpillars, and the starving kittens."

"Aren't you concerned about what will happen when you die?"

I said, "Only as concerned as I am for a pumpkin or a cow."

"But humans are different."

"Really?"

"There is the proof of Jesus."

"It is a wonderful story."

"It is more than a story."

I agreed, "Yes, more of a philosophy."

"The Truth. The Way. The Light."

I said, "The truth of the unknown."

Jamie said, "Yes!"

"The unknown is known? The unknown should be unknown, otherwise we should call it 'the known.'"

"Through grace the truth is known."

I said, "Yes, Katya told me the world has many truths of the unknown. Have you read the Books of Bokonon? The first verse explains a lot about my life, as Katya described it to me last night. I am now a subscriber."

"But only one truth is right, Johnny," he sighed. "You know what? This conversation is over."

Jamie was finished talking to me.

/* How I became weary with manuals through attrition, and the adoption of many adverbs. */

Just as a ladybug pulls in its limbs when you touch its shell, Jamie did so to me. From that moment on, he only talked of computers in my presence, and briefly at that, a misfortune, not just mine, but ours.

I collected my manuals from the coffee table. For the remainder of the day I studied Beamer WebCutter manuals. And the next day at work, I studied Beamer WebCutter manuals. And the day after that, the same. My manual habits stretched on for ninety days, during which time I had a weekly meeting with my manager where I made requests for an assignment, a bug, or anything to apply my stored knowledge to. The unceasing electrical whir was the sole stimuli to my sensory organs.

I asked my manager each week, "May I help you with a task? I have read so many manuals now. I'd like to begin an applicable project to my reading. Pardon me if I sound grumbling or plaintive."

The manager tilted his head to say, "Yes. Yes, I imagine the manuals have become tiring...if not fully a chore by now. Let me see. I've been very busy, and it is my regret not addressing this situation sooner." He pulled out a piece of paper to log my visit to his office. He pursed his lips and looked at the corner of the room.

He pondered, "What is today's date?" then he scribbled away for several minutes while my thumbs diddled brushily in the quietude of the whir.

Finally, he stopped writing, and said, "Let me see what we can figure out for you over the course of this week. By next week, I'll try to have something new for you."

I smiled and tilted my head, "I appreciate it."

He smiled a moment and stroked his moustache. He smiled, "How about those Green Bay Packers?"

"They surely are a fine team," I said in a lilted voice.

"They are doing quite well, but the season is really long, and certainly anything can happen," he tilted his head so that his ear reached his shoulder.

I replied, "How very true."

I started back to my office, careful to waste as little Beamer time and money as possible, but still dragging my feet so that I might vicariously peer into other Beamers' offices to behold the exciting bleeding-edge technology they were developing. Some Beamers faced their monitor with their hands folded, some held phone conversations, some chatted on an instant messenger, and some discussed the news or stock prices with another Beamer. I witnessed a plethora of policy violations in nearly every office.

As I approached my office, my feet dawdled ever more when the voices of Danny and Fillmore reached my ear. I heard Danny's opinion freely put forth:

"It is my belief," Danny was saying, "that a homeowner has every right to shoot an intruder. I would shoot an intruder until he was twice-dead, and then tell my lawyer, 'He was attacking me; it was self defense, you see.'"

Before I could even see Danny, I knew he was performing the *beachball->football->waiting-for-a-bird routine* with his hands. Making the turn into the office, the first thing I noticed was the large dimple in Danny's peanut chin. Fillmore moved her large mass an inch to allow me to be seated. I opened a manual to read, but they spoke loudly...

Danny went on, "If someone entered my car, I would shoot them. Private property."

Fillmore said, "Johnny, would you like to see some pictures?"

"Yes, please," I fibbed.

Danny said, "I'm not sure if he's old enough to see them. He's too young."

I asked Danny, "How old are you?"

"I'm twenty-four," he said.

I said, "I'm twenty-two."

"See, like I said, you are just a young pup. Fillmore, make sure you screen the pictures he looks at."

I smiled outwardly at Danny and thumbed through the pictures, all of which featured the cat Mr. Pococurante involved in standard feline activities.

Fillmore narrated, "Here's Mr. Pococurante on the couch. Isn't that adorable? And there's my husband holding a string out for Mr. Pococurante to play with. Here's Mr. Pococurante sleeping on the couch. Here he is washing himself..."

Danny said, "Washing himself? Don't let Johnny see that one. It's too lewd for him."

Fillmore continued, "And here's my husband sitting on my lap, with Mr. Pococurante sitting on his lap. It's our family picture."

I smiled, "It's a fine family photo." I tried not to express amusement when I saw the incredible size difference between Fillmore and her husband: the husband sat on Fillmore's lap like an elf might on Santa Claus.

Danny said, "Johnny, you should bring in pictures of your family. Oh, wait, I forgot - you're not married."

"That's correct, I am not connubial."

Danny said, "You probably cannot find anyone to marry you."

I smiled with plasticity, "That seems unnecessary to accuse me of. I see no great urgency for marriage."

Danny sneered, "That's what you *would* say."

I said, "Well, may I see a picture of your family, Danny?"

He produced a photo from his wallet that displayed what appeared as a collage of Danny the peanut head, an albino female ape, and a tiny goblin-child.

I smirked and tilted my head, "Yes, you have a handsome family, too, Danny."

"More so than yours," Danny badgered.

"A comparison does not exist," I sighed, "but if you insist."

Without another wasted response, feeling a certain level of chagrin, I started reading my manual once again. When Fillmore left our office that day, Danny and her continued their unending exchanges over the instant messenger, and Danny still relayed all they talked about verbally to me. In this workless manner, the days went forth. I yearned for anything to program, to design, to build. Mondays I found the office tolerable, Tuesdays manageable, Wednesdays cumbersome, Thursdays unwieldy, and Fridays lumbering. Each week the lumbering mood commenced earlier, and one week I felt as if a giant monster had wrapped its hand around my chest and squeezed my ribcage. The muscles in my shoulders started tightening, and my chest cavity felt strangely compressed. I did not know what to think of the condition, so I went on reading manuals while Danny read the news.

Danny whined, "Listen to this: 'Interest rates lowered again.' My bank had better match what this newspaper says or I will be shopping for a new bank. I'm sure they will come up with some excuse to screw me, or some way to pretend they cannot match the new rates. I'm going to call them right now. Johnny, did you hear me? Johnny?...are you ignoring me?"

/* How a squirrel in a birdbath allowed me to meet the divorcee across the street. */

At the end of one particular day, with my chest ratcheted fairly tight, I drove home at an immeasurable rate of speed, immeasurable only because my speedometer maxed out at one hundred. Though I knew my speed was reckless, my foot insisted on pushing the pedal with heavy force. When I reached my house, I noticed impressions on the steering wheel leather where my fingers had gripped, and my fingers themselves had adopted a bloodless hue.

Across the street stood a fine house, mirroring my own rental house in every structural facet except for the aluminum siding's tint and the addition of a birdbath to the front yard. Now in this birdbath a squirrel splashed, quite determined to take a noisy bath, and he scared off two loving mourning doves in the process. As soon as the squirrel landed in the water, from the front door came a charging attractive woman holding a broom, and she was exasperated with the rodent in her birdbath. She windmilled violently toward the birdbath seeking to wreak nothing short of death to the squirrel.

She yelled, "That's for the birds, not you! You lousy rat!"

The squirrel, with the attentiveness of his species, hopped to the ground and bounded into the neighbor's yard.

The woman yelled, "Now stay there!"

With that exclamation the woman turned back to her house to go indoor. But as soon as the front door shut behind her, the wily squirrel reappeared in the birdbath, and enjoyed himself without a shred of remorse. I saw the woman's face in a window of the house; it was a face of sheer revulsion. Her face jerked away from the window, and the front door spewed forth the broom-wielding woman once again. She was indeed an attractive woman with much to offer to a man's imagination, if he felt so inclined. The squirrel ran beyond the boundary of her yard once again. She ran to the edge of her own yard, then stopped as if unable to cross into the neighbor's lawn, and she scolded the plucky scofflaw, but the squirrel seemed not in the least bit intimidated or interested by her metaphorical scourging.

"You little pig!" she shouted, and doing so made me wonder how a squirrel would feel if he could understand that she had compared him to a pig and what might the squirrel have said in response.

Again, she went inside the house and again the scene reproduced itself, unabridged and unscripted; the squirrel bathed lackadaisically until she chased him with the fervor of an infernal Fury. My chest loosened as I allowed my bulging laughter to spill out of me and into the atmosphere. Upon hearing my laughter, the woman in pursuit blushed, stopped, and said shyly,

"That darn thing just won't leave the birdbath alone. I could shoot him."

And I said, "But he just wants to bathe. Methinks he would like to scrub behind his little ears."

"Methinks he can do it in a puddle."

"Methinks you might be right, too," I acquiesced.

She set her bristled weapon down and walked across the street toward me. A twinge of nervousness overcame me as she approached. Her strut radiated her feminine poetry: 'Her tawny legs in a brief pair of shorts / Her navel slightly exposed / Her breasts highlighted in red pinstripes / Her neck as soft as a rose.'

She said, "My name is Shawna."

"And I am Johnny Pepper."

She offered a delicate handshake.

She asked, "What are you reading?"

"Beamer manuals."

"Oh, so you are a Beamer?"

"I am a new Beamer," I said with pride.

"That's great," she smiled, "and what is your job?"

"I'm a software engineer, but so far I have engineered nothing."

"But you Beamers are paid very well, aren't you?"

I nodded, "Oh yes. We're paid top dollar."

"Mmm...that's interesting."

I asked, "What do you do, Shawna?"

"I am currently a housewife. My ex-husband is a construction worker. He works long days, especially in the summer months."

"Does he know about your squirrel problem?"

She sighed, "I don't think he'd care."

"Oh, no?"

"No, he wouldn't. Because we are divorced."

"That is a shame."

She said, "Not really."

I felt an imperative urge to change the subject. I said, "Although you have your opinion, I feel that the squirrel should be allowed to bathe."

"You think so, do you?"

"I do."

"And why is that?"

"He is a great source of entertainment."

"He is a nuisance."

I smiled, "But an entertaining nuisance."

She rolled her eyes, "I think you are the new source of entertainment around here. I'm going to keep my eye on you." She winked at me. "See you later, Johnny Pepper."

Shawna made one last enticing glance at me as she walked away brandishing her tight bottom in my direction, and my head mechanically followed each step's oscillation, like a sunflower does to the sun.

/* Finally, a bug to work on. But first, the red tape. */

After the ninety Beamer nights of manual constipation, I trudged to my office holding another manual under my arm. Reading became a constant sorrow as I struggled to get through a single page in twenty minutes. Danny and Fillmore seemed to accomplish no more than an hour of actual work each day given the persistence of their conversations, yet both of them received a raise from my manager, and both of them felt shortchanged. Beamer's frugality became a subject of consternation to them, and I listened facing away from them.

Danny said, "This raise is a fine example of poor management. Last year, my raise produced a ten percent gain, and this year only three percent."

Fillmore said, "How does Beamer expect to retain its good employees?"

Danny scoffed, "Oh, I've already been looking elsewhere for employment, somewhere that employees are rewarded for working hard. Beamer must expect performance without compensation; I am offended by this."

"They just do not appreciate people," Fillmore grieved. "Did you know that the warehouse workers just received a one dollar raise?"

Danny was shocked. "You see what I mean? That's more than a ten percent raise for them. And here we are, the engineers, receiving only three percent."

Fillmore added, "I bet our bonuses this year will be less than four thousand dollars apiece."

"How disgusting," Danny shook his head. "We do the

significant work and receive peanuts."

After several hours of listening to complaints, I tried to read another page of my Beamer WebCutter manual, but I only stared through the book, past the desk, and into a daydream. I shook loose of the trance in an attempt to concentrate, but found myself again drifting; dreaming of being an African lioness. I became her, as she feasted on a freshly slain gazelle, engorging herself with raw meat until she could eat no more, and when her belly grew full, she ate until she could no longer move, and when she could no longer move she laid on her side to gnaw the gazelle, and when she could no longer gnaw, she laid pathetically still and fell into a catatonic slumber of pain, without enjoyment. Then around the carcass, flies started to gather in orgiastic revelry. And the once beautiful ballet-bouncing gazelle became infused with maggot embryos. The daydream depressed me.

The following day Ted, my Beamer role model, showed up at my tiny office bearing good news. He offered me a bug. Internally, my organs leapt at the opportunity, thinking that my manual days had ended. A fresh vitality surfaced in me.

Ted said, "I bet you thought I forgot about you, huh Johnny?"

"No. No not at all!"

"I've been so busy with projects," he said apologetically. "How long has it been since I last talked to you?"

"A few months. But I have been reading manuals, preparing myself for an assignment."

"Well, you are in luck today," Ted smiled. "First we just have to get you logged in on a few systems. Let's try this. You should already have access I would think..."

My fingers bounced on the keyboard with liveliness in lieu of the awaiting code. I typed my username and password at the terminal prompt; I waited for my account to activate. Indeed, I could not imagine a better feeling at that moment. The terminal responded:

```
530 Login Incorrect.
Login failed
```

Ted scratched his head, "Oh. Well, you might need to sign up for access to this system. Try it again."

Carefully, I entered my username and password:

```
johnnypep
**********
```

We watched and waited. Danny and Fillmore turned to watch the outcome:

```
530 Login Incorrect.
Login failed
```

Ted said, "Well, well. I'll have to submit a request for access, and in a couple of days you should get an automated response. Sorry about that. You'll just have to wait."

As Ted left the office, Danny snickered, Fillmore whinnied, and I made one last unsuccessful attempt to log in.

For three Beamer nights I waited for access, even checking my e-mail at home to find out if my time had come to log in. On the fourth day, my account became a living creature.

```
331 User johnnypep ok.
230 -
230 Restricted user logged in.
```

An effervescent bubble percolated in me like a belch, and I whisked myself over to Ted's office, making only two wrong turns in the Beamer labyrinth before reaching his office, but he was not present. I waited an hour for him to return. When he returned I urged him to show me what next to do.

"Ok, let's go to your office," he said.

"Yes, right away."

Back in my office, Ted said, "Now we are getting somewhere. What you have to do next is run a script to setup your view to the WebCutter code. Type in 'beamview WebCutter 2345.iv.secIV.ver5 -gdmf' and see what happens."

I typed the script command and waited, more excited than before, more than ever...

```
File permissions do not allow access.
```

My heart sunk with the latest disclosure from my monitor. Ted pensively looked at the green output, considering what he had failed to consider.

"I remember now," Ted admitted, "You have to get access to another machine first. Sorry about that, Johnny. I forgot all about that other server. Let me submit a request for that machine. I hope we can get all of these things fixed for you, without you becoming too bored."

I smiled half-heartedly, "I am just excited to be moving along."

He said, "You can read manuals in the meantime, I guess. There isn't much else you can do but wait."

My heart sunk further. Ted walked away. Three Beamer nights later, I was allowed to run the script - it ran successfully, I had access to the code, so I thought, until I went one step further and received another senseless message:

```
Type not found.
```

Once again, Ted pensively looked at my monitor, and decided I needed additional software installed, so I went to download the software. But the downloading site decided that I needed to submit a licensing request to my manager, but my manager had just left the country on a business trip, and would not return to Minneapolis for a week. So for seven more Beamer nights little happened, with the only exception being my partaking in the world of instant-messaging with co-workers, constituting my first violation of Beamer policy. I felt ashamed, at first, to be out of line with the well-established and defined policies, but after observing so many other Beamer employees in violation, I rationalized that instant-messaging at work was no worse than telling a white lie. Besides that, the instant connectivity of Beamer allowed us to become closer to one another. Across all boundaries, across the world, across the hall; how amazing technology is. The Korean fellow who sat across the hall from my office started a discussion with me one day, and we chatted for the whole week, and most amazingly, through the duration of this conversation he and I never once were forced to leave our offices for any face-to-face conversation.

When my manager finally returned from his business trip, my mind had forgotten the licensing request altogether until an e-mail came to me, informing me that the software I needed was now available. I installed the software under Ted's direction, and finally had access to the elusive code.

Ted said, "You may have noticed - Beamer has a lot of red-tape. It's a shame it took this long to get you logged in to the right places."

"Yes."

"But here you are, Johnny. Here is a description of the bug. I'll just let you get started. Good luck! Stop by anytime if you have questions."

* * * * *

After Ted left, Danny said, "You know what you need?"

I said, "No, what?"

"Some lipstick. So you can pucker up a little more when you kiss Ted's ass."

I said, "Danny, at the very least I am thrilled to do some work. You seem more caught up in conversation than work."

Danny scoffed, "I'm working. That's exactly what I am

doing right now: work. See?"

Danny showed me the same files he had showed me on my first day at Beamer.

With that, I turned away from Danny to read the description of my precious bug that I had to fix. This, I felt, held the solution to all my frustration. All my pent up creative energy at last had an outlet to uncontain itself upon. The bug description started with the following and had another two hundred pages of log files to go with it:

```
'Missing native pointer error' seg fault
Beamer WebCutter on systems set to German
locale. Occurs on creation of a date on
save. Segmentation Fault (Core Dumped).
Last logged information file follows:

2/1 05:36:55 PM    Testing Date() GMT CDT
German International

2/1 05:36:55 PM    Insert measure()

2/1 05:36:55 PM    Proc conv.

2/1 05:36:55 PM    d  = Mar 23 16:31:15 UTC
2000

2/1 05:36:56 PM    dp = Mar 23 11:31:15 UTC
2000

2/1 05:36:56 PM    equals()

2/1 05:36:56 PM    null

2/1 05:36:56 PM    dp = Mar 23 10:30:15 AM
UTC 2000
```

2/1 05:36:56 PM d = Mar 23 03:30:15 PM UTC 2000

2/1 05:36:56 PM Inoperable proc attempted not found.

2/1 05:36:56 PM Inoperable proc attempted not found.

2/1 05:36:56 PM Inoperable proc attempted not found.

2/1 05:36:56 PM Missing native pointer violation.

2/1 05:36:56 PM Server initiating shutdown.

2/1 05:36:56 PM ###### Server Failed. Producing last known info. ######

.340982340a(*)*)8243533499980 989 ASDK

.STACK sent to log file.

.Line 5629 last execution in file xoverunder convchart listless.c

.Last executed lines:

```
BmDast         *         activeSpot       =
bm_sdk_init_first(INIT_DATE(init_opt_sdk(IT
EM_STARBOARD(file_alpha))));

Bm_Xup * xup_1 = broke_static<Bm_Xup *>
(up_negsig);
```

/* How I came to walk in an ocean one inch deep all over. */

The computer mouse felt more like a live bird in my hand as I searched for the first file of C++ code. My fingers writhed like Medusa's hair as I typed commands to traverse the file system, and in a short time I had wandered into a panoramic bliss of code that extended for a million lines in all directions, as Ted had promised. In my initial fervor, I soon had opened twenty files for viewing, with the absurd hope of rousting an immediate solution to the bug. But after a few hours of direct searching, the approach failed miserably.

So I attempted to reproduce the bug, expecting the nature of the problem to become patent. Here my ardent study of the Beamer manuals finally found a usage. I retraced the steps of the customer who discovered the bug, but unlike the customer, my computer did not crash. Instead, my computer worked perfectly fine. I grunted my confusion. Danny had been watching me over my shoulder. I felt his fetid breath on my shirt collar when he said, "What are you doing?"

After shuddering, I said, "Attempting to reproduce the customer's bug, as I'm sure you can see that as well as I can from how close you are."

Danny's neck stretched forward further, putting his peanut head right next to mine, such that if my head turned, we would have kissed. Danny moved his chair closer, not that the office allowed much movement, and he offered his unsolicited help in solving my bug. His teeth chomped metrically while he read my computer screen.

He said, "You need to set your WebCutter up to use the German language."

I said, "But I do not speak German."

"You do now."

Befuddled, I asked, "Who will interpret the German?"

"No one. You will. You'll have to set up an English WebCutter on another machine to watch the German server's output next to the English server's output, side-by-side. Understand? Am I speaking too fast for you? You have to watch one monitor showing English, and one monitor showing German."

I asked, "But where will I get another computer? May I use your machine?"

"Absolutely not. I have too many work items on my plate as it is. I don't need to be taking on your work as well."

"How do I make my WebCutter speak German?"

"Hey, I'm not the all-knowing Beamer here. You'll have to figure it out. I'm sure it's simple enough to do."

Simply enough I spent the remainder of the day uninstalling, reinstalling, downloading, and butchering files until finally, the bug crashed my server using the German language. The Beamer offices were all empty when I left my office. I had not noticed the time passing. I lost track of time in the windowless, weatherless, lifeless office. On the drive home that night, under the freeway lights, I wanted to stop somewhere for a drink but I went straight home, to bed, so that I might arrive early to debug the Germanic blight.

The morning alarm sounded, I burst out of my bedsheet with my bare body, and dressed for Beamer rapidly. I expected to be the last to leave work, and the first to arrive. I wanted to be the early bird getting the worm; to be high-speed with low-drag.

After I raced to work, I started the debug session right away, determined to solve the problem, post-haste, determined to harpoon a digital whale.

I logged in and, still highly motivated, stared wild-eyed into the code.

Looking hard with beady eyes, I read through lines of code expecting the answer to jut out at me. On and on for hours, page after page, thousand of lines, where-oh-where! My wild eyes went from fire to cold stone. I felt naked wandering in the WebCutter abyss. The old programmer left not a single comment for me to identify with. All was senseless. I needed Ted's tutelage.

When Ted noticed me in the doorway, he said, "Johnny, I expected to see you sooner or later. I wanted to see how far you would get on that bug."

"Then I have failed."

Ted laughed, "Oh please. Not at all. Remember I told you about the enormity of this WebCutter product? And you have only seen a limb of the code body so far. You will never see all of it. Never. It is an ocean one inch deep all over."

"An ocean one inch deep all over?"

Ted sipped on his venti-size coffee. "That's the best description I can think of. You can see for miles and miles while standing on the surface of this ocean, but to understand anything you have to walk around with your head down and look at each square foot. However, you'll be glad to know you can place yourself anywhere in the ocean at any time. You can find the proper starting place for each bug."

I admitted, "I'm afraid you will have to show me the starting place."

Ted warned me, "Do not let cluelessness degrade your attitude. Programmers need a certain zeal for confusion. Debuggers especially feel partially clueless every day, largely because they are repairing code written by someone else years ago."

"From 1975."

"Goodness, is some of it that old? Whoever wrote the original WebCutter code is retired by now. Of course, much of the initial code was written for other projects, long before the existence of the internet. Obviously, much of the code is fairly new, I assure you. Let's go to your office and I'll show you a few techniques I use."

I said, "Academia is much cleaner than Beamer."

Ted agreed, "No doubt about it. But college is meant to prepare you for these types of horrific environments by laying foundations of problem solving. In this occupation you need to be conventional and abstract. If you force yourself into rigidity, you lose creativity. On the other hand, if you try to lasso the moon with every line of code you write, you will become an unproductive fool. Try to foster your creativity with engineering between the pylons of convention and concoction. If you follow that rule you'll be designing applications within five years. By the way, where did you go to college?"

"Bildungsroman University."

"Oh yes," Ted nodded, "they have as fine a curriculum as anywhere. Did you spend much time around the Perineum?"

"Oh yes, as much as possible, but not nearly as much as I would have liked."

"North or south side?"

"The north side."

"Oh, too bad. Follow me."

Ted spent an hour explaining the approaches he used in debugging. I scribbled down all that he said and nodded unceasingly, as an unquestioning apostle. As Ted looked at the code written by previous Beamers, he commented on the lack of quality in the code. He harped on the importance of every line to be of uniform style and convention, saying that programming requires detail, and that spending an additional five minutes on a section of code makes a programmer look wise. He said that the appearance, placement, and comments a programmer uses is as important as plumb, level, and flush is to a concrete mason. Esoteric or muddled code needs recognition and rectification. All wasted lines of code and unnecessary use of space shows how unskilled a programmer is.

"It's hard to believe, Johnny," Ted said, "that many Beamers spend twenty-five years writing bad code." Ted pointed at the monitor, "This file right here is where you should start trying to fix this particular bug."

"Thank you."

"Keep in mind that the starting point is not a magic bullet. This is where the crash occurred, then you work backwards from here."

"And the German?"

"Yes, debugging in foreign languages will take a while to get used to, but you will learn to debug without looking at the server output at all. International software presents a whole new arena of bugs, so have fun with it. You don't need to learn German to debug. If you get stuck again, come see me."

As a caterpillar must yearn when it looks upon a

butterfly, so did I admire Ted.

Danny arrived at his usual time, two hours after the recommended arrival time. As if Fillmore could smell when Danny he arrived, she soon showed her face in our office and butted her way passed me to her narrow stable. Together, they watched my every move, adding commentary as I worked. But with zest I debugged, if only to make them jealous.

"Must be nice," Danny said to me, "to have one of the senior engineers holding your hand. I wish I had the job you've been assigned to."

I smiled at my monitor listening to his gripe.

From then the days wore on, from early mornings, to late nights, to short lunches, and to dog fights with the debugger. Even with Ted's techniques I had to look through hundreds of thousands of lines, down a thousand wrong rabbit holes. Always, I came back to study the same lines, almost positive the answer hid within somehow:

```
BmDast          *         activeSpot          =
bm_sdk_init_first(INIT_OPT(init_opt_sdk(ITE
M_STARBOARD(file_alpha))));

Bm_Xup  *  xup_1  =  broke_static<Bm_Xup  *>
(up_negsig);
```

Two weeks of my life went by as I exhausted every idea I had for a solution. The bug that promised to be my saving grace from boredom drove me to utter confusion. Danny giggled each time I swore under my breath. I looked for something to blame.

Germany. I started to blame Germany for the bug. The

struggles of the world against Germanic peoples throughout history came to mind - The Goths, the Prussians, the Nazis...and wasn't Charlemagne Germanic, too? Well, it doesn't matter if he was. To hell with him too. What were the Germans planning to do with this software anyway? Could it be anything positive? Was mankind better off if I didn't fix this bug? Lederhosen...Sauerkraut...Auschwitz.

Then I shifted my disparaging thoughts from Germany to the old Beamer programmer who had sown this very bug years ago. Was his retirement treating him well? What color was his parachute? Surely golden. Surely he was sipping on gin drinks with baby umbrellas in some Florida senior-living Bedpan Manor. Surely he reminisced on the quality of product he produced while at Beamer. Surely he claimed his own excellence in writing code and denounced the professionalism of today's young people. Surely he was fully bloated with complaints about the younger generation's disrespect for elders. What a lunatic the man was...concerned only with his own affairs of drunken pedantry and hedonic splurging of his 401K, his pension. He was to blame. He was probably German, too. The sick son of a...

But during my criticism, I came across a technical document online that opened my eyes to the nature of the code failure. In an obscure website, owned by a competitor of Beamer, I read these words carefully, and slowly:

```
"For this data structure, an interface
pointer is a pointer to a pointer. This
pointer points to an array of pointers,
each of which points to an interface
function."
```

Could it be true? Each pointer points to an array of pointers?

This illuminating fact was a treasure: A pointer to a

pointer, that points to an array of pointers, and, of course, each pointer in the array of pointers points to an interface function pointer. Epiphany! What simplicity, in the end. The Nazi Hedonist programmer deserved some praise after all. He wrote very clever code (though not at all intuitive). And now I could fix the bug for the good people of Germany (where I decided would be a wonderful place to visit someday).

So patience is a debugging virtue. Solving the bug required delicate patience, similar to how one goes about catching a fuzzy that wafts through the air. The quicker and harder you throw out your hand trying to snatch the fuzzy from the air, the easier the fuzzy evades your hand. Instead, by following and watching and waiting on the fuzzy, it comes to rest in your palm.

I kissed my monitor on the lips in appreciation, and to make apologies for my earlier cursing. I looked again at the lines:

```
BmDast         *         activeSpot         =
bm_sdk_init_first(INIT_OPT(init_opt_sdk(ITE
M_STARBOARD(file_alpha))));

Bm_Xup  *  xup_1  =  broke_static<Bm_Xup  *>
(up_negsig);
```

And in there I could see the obvious point of failure. I changed the code to this:

```
BmDast         *         activeSpot         =
bm_sdk_init_first(INIT_OPT(init_opt_sdk(ITE
M_STARBOARD(file_alpha))));
```

```
Bm_Xup   *   xup_1   =   broke_static<Bm_Xup>
(up_negsig);
```

I patched my pointers and recompiled, rebuilt the program, and everything worked in German and English. I e-mailed the nice German customers, telling them I had found a solution. I felt so excited I decided to tell Danny and Fillmore about the fix.

"Guess what? I figured out the problem with the code! You know what happened? The German system opened a file using a null string, but the English systems used an assumed environment variable, resulting in a pointer exception due to a template..."

"Well it took you long enough. I would hope you are done."

Fillmore said, "Great. You should get started on the next bug right away. We have so many to fix, and I could assign a few of mine to you."

I went on, "But this is really amazing. The bug crashed the server because of these pointers to pointers here, in this line of code..."

"Oh yeah, that's amazing all right, but so is this," Danny interjected. "Listen to this Fillmore: '*Code Red Mountain Dew* to be marketed soon.' Good God all-mighty. Is that the best name they could come up with? I mean, how many marketing PhD's did they have to hire for that stroke of genius. Pfft!"

My excitement ended abruptly.

/* The Beamer night I solved the bug. */

I felt an itch inside my brain that turned out to be a craving to see Katya. The bug had monopolized my time for the past weeks making me negligent in calling her. An urgency pervaded my spirit to celebrate with her in any way she would allow. Danny left work at three o'clock in the afternoon, putting in his usual five hours of work (with a one hour lunch). After Danny left, I decided to leave a little early, in celebration of conquering my first Beamer bug.

I dialed Katya and talked fast into the phone. I said, "Katya, hello, it's me Johnny Pepper, and I am intent on picking you up for a date, if you would enjoy my company. I would enjoy your company enormously."

"Tonight?" she said.

I said, "Ok, tonight works well for me. Shall I meet you around five o'clock?"

"Five...?" she said.

"Yes, five works well for me, too. I'll see you then, Katya, my beautiful tulip of the city, my dainty flower in the Minneapolis mud!"

She said, "Flattery becomes quickly annoying, Johnny."

"I only flatter one woman. My Katya Katyavich."

"Oh wow. That's probably enough of that. I could meet you at six o'clock."

The clock clung to the minutes as I waited for six o'clock. To pass the time I looked out the front window of the house at the quiet street where no movement or change occurred until a truck pulled into the driveway across the street to where the divorcee, Shawna, lived. Shawna came outside to greet the man in the truck, who was a man of large servings. The dusty boots made a cloud around him when he stepped out of the truck to engage Shawna in a conversation that I could not quite hear. She appeared as lovely as before, with fine clothes on her body that hugged every curve. The fact that the man divorced her seemed preposterous when surely many other men waited like dogs for attention from women like her. Yearning to listen in on the discussion, I decided to walk out of my front door and pretend to check the oil in my car.

The burly man said, "Well, I'll tell you why I came home early, if you'd just let me speak…"

Shawna said, "You've had your chance to speak. You should have called or said something earlier in the week if you wanted to try amending."

"Amending what? I've done nothing…"

"Don't give me that old line! You blew me off too many times before," Shawna said sternly. "Besides, I already have plans to go out with my girlfriends tonight. So whatever you had in mind, you can stick it right back where you pulled it out of!"

The man tried to calm her. "Please, keep your voice down. I wanted to take you to a play at the Guthrie theater tonight…but…forget it. I don't need this. Every time I try to do something nice you just…"

She pointed her finger in his face, "Like when you stayed out last weekend fishing, and left me here? Like when you work until 8:00 at night, and then come home and watch the Twins and pass out."

"But I work the long hours for us, baby. So we can have nice things in a few years. I'm not trying to hurt you…"

"Oh, spare me the details." Shawna held one of her hands in the air, and chopped at the space between them. "So on top of your neglect, you are a liar. What's next? Are you gay?"

The husband stood silent for a bit, put one foot in the truck, then his other foot, then backed out of the driveway to exit the scene. Seeing this development, I turned to enter my house, but Shawna yelled, "Hey Johnny Pepper: do you see what a thug that man is?"

I ran inside to hide, pretending not to hear Shawna.

To kill time I decided to look out the rear window of the house where nothing controversial would draw my attention. A tree sat still in the air, all alone, until a bluejay fluttered in to perch on a branch. And here, thought I, is true beauty. How beautiful the bluejay is, how bright and sweet, pecking his way along in life using only his beak and two feet, causing no trouble to anyone, simply adding comeliness to the outdoor scenes. He bobbled his head as he strutted around calmly and confidently. What more honest is there than beauty? What more serene?

A pair of sparrows landed quietly, in the same tree as the bluejay.

The bluejay cocked his head to one side, cock, cock, cock. Then he screamed and spread his wings. He flew directly at the little sparrows, who did not have time to react due to the speed and proximity of the bluejay. The sparrows spread their little wings to make an attempt at escape. One sparrow swooped south, one flapped north. The former escaped while the latter met the bluejay's beak. The bluejay beak punched the sparrow in the wing and knocked out a plume of sparrow feathers. The sparrow fell to the earth stunned, injured, as his own feathers snowed around him, sadly. And proudly sat the bluejay on the branch where the sparrows had been. He still looked beautiful in a way, but ugly, too.

At last, the time came to meet Katya, in the Twin Cities location called Dinkytown. My feet slapped the pavement as I traversed the sidewalk in pursuit of Katya. I cruised up and down, slapping away at the sidewalk squares, back and forth, up and down, finding many restaurants and bars, but no Katya. Like a child, I made sure not to step on the sidewalk cracks. Then a voice said,

"Johnny Pepper, would you quit walking around with your head down? I've watched you walk by three times now. I'm right here!"

I looked up from my foot-slapping. "There you are. I looked everywhere!"

"You looked everywhere on your shoes," Katya laughed.

"I don't like to step on cracks." I looked Katya up and down. "You look beautiful as ever. As you always do, I'm certain."

"Thank you. You should back off the flattery. Try bringing flowers or something less patronizing."

I smiled, "And when you are the most beautiful tulip, what flower could I bring to match thee?"

"Good night! Do you ever expect that crap to work on a woman?"

"Only on one woman."

I looked out the window and tried to think of something to say, but the German bug had monopolized my mind for so long that I thought of little else.

"You know," I said, "I've been so busy at Beamer lately, that my mind is swimming in work even now. During sleep, even, I'm locked into a programming situation. When I left work, all I could think of was seeing you tonight, and now my tongue cannot think of anything to ask you. How is that for irony?"

She said, "That's not irony. That's distraction. Or maybe just unfortunate."

"Oh? Then what would be ironic?"

"Let's see," she furrowed her brow. "Maybe if you had been uncontrollably excited to see me so you drove really fast to get here and on the last turn your brakes failed and your car ran through the intersection and crashed into this restaurant and mortally wounded me - that would be pretty ironic."

I nodded, "Wouldn't that be unfortunate?"

"It would for me. And you, since you'd have to miss work at Beamer for court proceedings as to your own negligence."

I said, "Negligence! No thank you. I've seen what happens to the negligent. And I would hate to miss work. I love Beamer."

She said, "I can tell that you love it. What do you love about Beamer?" she asked.

The answer seemed too obvious for words. I said, "Is this a trick question? Who wouldn't want to be a Beamer?"

"I wouldn't want to be, believe it or not."

A response came to me, gathered from the information taught to me during Beamer orientation. I said, "Beamer makes the world a better place by increasing the standard of living for everyone. Beamer connects the globe digitally, allowing everyone in the world to exploit technology equally. Beamer has led the corporate world in hiring women and employees of diverse backgrounds. Beamer respects all employees and treats them well. Those are some of the reasons I love Beamer. Do you disagree?"

Katya paused before saying, "I don't want to be a sower of discord to you, or damage your positive attitude. Your optimism is inspiring, honestly."

"Don't you agree that Beamer has increased the standard of living for the world, or at least Americans?"

"I'd rather not answer," she said.

"No, go ahead," I said, "I want to hear what your viewpoint is."

"Ok, Johnny. I'll answer, but remember this is just my opinion. Ok?"

"Fine. Go ahead, I'm always excited to hear a new opinion."

Katya sat back in her chair to get comfortable. She said, "Beamer makes the 'standard' of living better for Beamers, not everyone. Who defines the 'standard of living'? Is a good standard of living having a lush lawn? Is a high standard of living driving a nice car for an hour a day in traffic to where you live, away from the social problems you indirectly support? Is a high standard of living having health insurance so you can afford Prozac just to get through your life? In case you haven't noticed, Americans are more depressed than anyone, and to me that indicates a lowered standard of living. And I don't believe that Beamer has extended business across the globe for humanitarian reasons. Beamer's goal is a fiscal goal, and will always be fiscal. In order to perpetually increase sales and revenue, Beamer will squeeze the globe like an orange until it's dry."

In case other Beamers were dining in the restaurant at the same time and hearing Katya, I shrunk in my seat. I felt off guard and responded quietly.

I said, "What about Beamer's donations to charities and extension of opportunities to nations and people that otherwise have no ladder to success? Certainly, with women and minorities, Beamer helped lead the way in those areas."

Katya replied, "Do you really think that Beamer started those practices as goodhearted gestures?"

"Absolutely!"

"Any action Beamer takes in areas of tolerance is done to increase the wealth of the company. They started diverse hiring practices to increase their bottom line, not for altruistic reasons. Forward thinking businessmen find an edge. They wanted the best engineers, that's all. Everyone is a customer, Johnny. It's screw or be screwed. The business of business is business. Ethics is the best way to lose. After I worked in pharmaceutical sales for three years and pushed the pills to meet sales quotas, I realized I'd chosen a career that didn't fit me."

I sat soaking her words in, feeling sure that she was missing a chromosome or gland of some kind. She took a drink of water and continued.

"The same company that ruins the lake with pollution will leave the mess until cleaning it can boost their public image, then they slap up a billboard to herald its corporate conscience. Advertising is truth."

I said, "But Beamer does so many more good things than bad. Think of diversity…"

"I knew we shouldn't have gotten started on this. I'm sorry Johnny. What we end up celebrating is diversity all right, but it's the diversity of wealth, not people. If Beamers wanted to celebrate diversity, then why do Beamers move away from every social problem? Instead of trying to escape the problems by moving away, maybe they should be moving toward the bad parts of the city. Perhaps the Beamers should put their 'good' kids into the 'bad' schools. Wouldn't the good kids have a positive effect on the bad kids, or don't Beamers trust their children? They want to make a buck and retire early and they don't care. Piss on society, that's what they say. By the way, if you can't tell, I grew up poor."

A waitress came to the table and said, "Are you ready to order?"

Growing angry, I whispered to Katya, "Beamers are not like that, and you are a damn Communist!"

The waitress said, "Perhaps you need a few moments?"

Katya said, "Oh no, I'll have the Club Sandwich. How very Beamer of you to accuse me of that, Johnny. I am a bit of a Pinko. But I'm not a Communist, I'm a concerned Capitalist."

The only thing I was certain of was that she was entirely wrong.

Katya said, "I don't expect you to agree with me, Johnny, and I'm not trying to convert you away from loving your job, but you asked my opinion. And I've learned that opinions on social issues should never get in the way of friendships or relationships."

As I got up to leave, I bumped into the waitress. I said, "I think I had better go home now. Perhaps we should not see each other anymore, Katya. I cannot believe...*you*."

Katya said as I left, "Well, have a nice life. It was nice getting to know you."

I slinked out the door, hoping no Beamers saw me leave.

Pete Flies

/* How I became rather competent, despite my grinding dreams, stiffening chest, and Danny's condescension at the lunch table. */

Reeling from Katya's apparent lunacy, I returned home and went to bed early, with the intention of rising with the birds so that I could fly off to work and tackle a new bug. During the night, my dreams turned to the madness of debugging in my sleep. Whether to be considered a dream or nightmare, these dreams became a common occurrence in the coming months. Programming streamed through my head in long lines, too fast, too long, too much for me to comprehend. Lines of code zinged by on a black screen with green text, from left to right, right to left, top to bottom, diagonal, and gone forever once I'd seen them.

So often in the dreams I'd grind my teeth trying to keep up with the code, and as I struggled to see each line, I would invariably catch a glimpse of a line exiting my field of vision. A certainty came over me that I had just missed the bit of code I needed to solve the problem. Then I would wake up, and grab at a pen and paper to write down the code I thought I had seen, with the hope of solving the problem. The dream had no solution, or no definition for that matter.

In the dreams, occasionally I would hear a lawnmower start right when the line I needed to see appeared in front of me. The lawnmower noise impeded my concentration. A pair of hands in white gloves (with no body attached) pushed a ghostly lawnmower along the code I was trying to read. The mower rolled along on the black screen over the bright green text, shearing off the tops of the words. Invariably in the dream, as my eyes neared the most important code, the lawnmower sheered the tops of the text off like grass, leaving only stumps of alphanumeric characters, making the rest of the dream an agony of replaying the slicing of the characters. Whatever the method my mind used to torment me on a given night of dreaming, I was assured to never reach the line of code that I sought, and the enamel of my teeth grew thin as time went on.

In my eagerness to arrive at work each day, I left the house at the same time the sun peeked over the horizon. If I arrived to work at 5:00 AM, I could still work ten or twelve hours or more and be home at a reasonable hour. What did I have to concern myself with other than work? Since Katya had made herself clear on wanting to destroy the Beamer way of life, I had no choice but to further it. A man can certainly accomplish many things in a day if he is lonely. Yet I thought of her with fondness on a daily basis, sometimes multiple times.

Every new bug I encountered quickly became an exercise in total confusion, frustrating me to no end. Ted saw more of my face than I imagine he wanted to, but he cordially answered my questions, no matter how mundane or obvious some of them must have seemed to him. Indeed, my attempts to solve the bugs were not halfhearted; I spent hours and days beating my head hoping for Serendipity's respite to come to me. Only after I exhausted my efforts would I ask Ted for assistance. My chest tightened during the bug-solving process each time until I found the solution, until the Beamer WebCutter customer e-mailed his thank you to me.

This tightening of the chest occurred primarily while I sat waiting for something to happen on my computer. I often felt tempted to surf the internet, but I refrained due to my compliance with Beamer policy. For every ten minutes of actual work, I generally had fifteen minutes of waiting for a stalled cursor or mouse to become active once processing finished. I stared with hate into my monitor, often cursing the dead screen, and blaming the monitor for network and server bottlenecks.

However, my diligence generated the birth of my competence. During this phase of confusion and slumping into Ted's office, I breached the learning curve and became proficient, much more so than Danny and Fillmore.

I started attending lunch with Danny, Fillmore, and their cronies. The lunchroom gymnasium buzzed with Beamerspeak as Beamers fed their brains with nourishment. The idea of Beamers eating food to produce programming languages tickled me. The apples they swallowed...transformed into files. The hamburgers...produced hardware. Fillmore, Danny, and I filled our trays with food from the large selection of entrees and joined the regular lunch group of Beamers. I exchanged pleasantries with all and uncomfortably began eating amidst them. The silence at our table often dominated the buzzing of all the other Beamers eating around us. Danny discussed his complaints as loudly at lunch as in the office. For example, one day he explained that he was working on running a test using a file, but, as he said,

"...the customer had only sent me the class files that were failing using our API. The customer didn't send me the source code. So right away I knew - these guys are idiots. I e-mailed again asking for the source code. But, of course, they didn't have the source. In fact, no one had the source code, and the guy who wrote the source had quit and went to another company, understandably. Who would work at a place where they allowed such ignorant people to manage technology?"

The Beamers laughed. Fillmore nodded. She'd already heard the story from Danny in the office.

"So now I'm sitting here with this error that I can't fix. I might as well go home."

Tentatively (for I always spoke softly at the table) I told Danny that he could use a certain technique, called a decompile, that would reconstruct the source code. He scoffed.

"You can't do that with this code."

But I said, "Hmm, I'm pretty sure you can." I spoke politely, acting as if unsure, even though I used this technique and knew that it worked fine.

"Well, I doubt it," said Danny. "Besides, that's not what my job is here. I'll tell you what Johnny, I'll forward the problem to you right away. It's all yours. Just let me know. Is that what you want? I got a bunch of other stuff you can work on, too. Anyway, I already told the customer that they are out of luck. I'm not going to baby-sit them."

The Beamers laughed at me and I laughed, too. At this point, I prayed that Danny become infected with syphilis. Oh, how upsetting some lunches were with him, with his peanut head so pale and white, and that dimple in the middle of his chin...disgusting to look at when added to his confidence...and his matted down hair in an attempted comb-over on his receding hairline...and his trendy eyeglasses...with his partial lisp. I despised how he mocked me and the other lunch nerd, a pitiful stuttering sap who wore Coke-bottle glasses. Because Danny was married to a mannish woman and the rest of us young Beamers only dated, Danny felt free to comment on our own personal relationships as if his skills with women were Byronesque. (To my pleasure, meeting his wife in person fulfilled my hopes and expectations: she was a horrible kind of Shrek.) Danny looked as geeky as the rest of us. Together we all looked disheveled and unnecessary, like a group of blemished products.

Throughout the lunch period the theme of all conversation clung to technology, such as our gizmos at home, Star Wars, fantasy lands and dragons, and the business world of technology. I shared little in the conversation, not for lack of knowledge, but for ambivalence toward the topics. Danny knew less than the others, but his opinions were always the most outspoken. His endless parade of scorn daggered at my ears.

When lunch ended, Danny led Fillmore and I back to the office taking an excessively long route through the winding halls of Beamer. He walked through labs, to the Beamer store, he stopped to read bulletin boards, and generally wasted time to avoid work. He looked out of windows to appraise the weather conditions. Even I lingered at the window a bit long because it was the only time I could see outside during the day.

Once we finally arrived at our desks, I felt my chest tightened merely from listening to Danny. Usually, returning to work to sit down pleased me...until Danny did the daily post-lunch ritual...of parking his greasy head beside mine, next to my ear where I could feel and smell his hot and sickening breath...

"So what are you working on now?" he exhaled.

And then I would turn and see Danny's head with his mealy-mouth gaping and catch a whiff of the residual lunch crumbs caught in his fangs.

/* How I discovered the Shittoon, learned of the necessary tragedies of the new economy, and daydreamed about a bull. */

As it is unavoidable for human beings to spend long periods of time in one place without eventually having the physical need to emit waste, such happened to me at Beamer. During my career as a Beamer, I never grew fully accustomed to the bathroom culture. Most Beamer bathrooms had a long series of consecutive bathroom stalls, usually occupied by silent Beamers. Various times I searched the many bathrooms that I knew of hoping to find a stool not in use. So many stools. So many Beamers in the act of stooling. There they sat. When I finally found a vacant stool, I sat down in silence. We all sat in silence, praying that somebody flushed, or turned on a faucet, or dried his hands - anything to make a noise so we could grab our next piece of toilet paper and quickly take a swipe at our anuses, and hope not to offend anyone else by the sound of toilet paper digging in our crevices. Using this method of slow wiping, or dragging rather, we attempted to minimize the audible sounds involved with stooling, but this slow dragging made the sound much worse than if we had just went about our business like our grandparents did, grunting and all. And not only was the wiping noise kept to a minimum; this courtesy also applied to the initial pushing and emitting as well, of which anyone knows that has ever pooped knows that trying to control the speed and sound will only inflict pain, inconsistency, and discontent on the colon. Sometimes a Beamer in the act of stifling couldn't hold it in any longer and he would let loose an explosive sound that disgusted and at the same time elated us all, as if yelling, 'At last!' At times I felt it would be less offensive if I'd simply stooled in my pants and called it a done deal, thus avoid the chore of having to adhere to the silent culture of Beamer bathrooms.

The culture made me wonder about Beamers as a population. Why the concern for the number two? What happened to the days when a man could stool with no doors on the stall, or the days when men had discussions while they stooled? Perhaps – can it be – that as a nation we have become fearful of our own rears?

Of course, some bathrooms were equipped with only one stall and several urinals, thereby seating only one stooler at a time. In these smaller bathrooms, the stall was situated so that upon entering and exiting the stall the stooler would be seen immediately by those standing at the urinals, and that lone stooler had to bear the burden of being the only stinker. In addition to this implicit accusation of stench, the acoustics of the smaller bathroom amplified the sound of emitting and wiping.

It so happened that one day I found all of my regular haunts occupied with like minded men, and I was pressed to go off in a frenzied search for a new stool to sit on. After lunch was always a difficult time to find a place to stool. That day I pioneered hallways untouched by my rear and stumbled into a large bathroom with two different sides separated by a partition. One side had the typical bathroom - with urinals, stalls, and sinks - but the other side housed a design far better; a single handicapped stall occupied the entire side. Yes, one luxurious handicapped stall and one sink. As I toured the handicapped side, I realized then that handicapped stalls are the Cadillac of all stools. Not only is the handicapped stall spacious, but it also treats all people, disabled or not, with a great deal of privacy. It is a modern marvel. The sole drawback to the handicapped stall is the frequency of which the seat can be found littered with urine, or on certain dark days, actual remnants of another man's solids. But cleaning the toilet seat is a small price to pay for such privacy, away from all the other miming mudslingers. No one could even see my feet under the door when I sat down.

I named this little piece of heaven: 'The Shittoon.'

The Shittoon reminded me of a cabin of solitude, a place of meditation, where not a wire of technology or Beamerdom existed, where I could wipe at will and flush my problems down the great whirling hole that brings all Americans' fecal matter together.

On my initial usage of the Shittoon, I remained inside for an hour, dreaming of adventures I might engage in if the Shittoon were a boat. I'd travel the seven seas sailing the Shittoon.

"Man the gunwale, bring up more cannon fodder. Listen up men: today you fight for freedom and candid wiping! For bowel comfort! You fight for the Shittoon!!"

As I enjoyed this scenario, two men entered the bathroom, and I overheard their conversation despite the partition. I listened to them until finally I was able to drift off into another daydream.

A man with a deep voice said, "Oh yeah, the word is out again. They are talking twenty-five percent of the work force this time. I even heard someone talk of the whole site getting shut down."

A higher voice said, "That's just hearsay. I've heard that same rumor twenty times in my career here. It won't be that big of a deal, believe me."

The deep voice said, "Why then? Why this continual rumor of fear? Every two months I hear the same rumor."

High said, "But it will just be a vendor layoff. It's no dig deal."

Then I realized that the Deeper voice was a new Beamer, like myself, asking questions to the Higher voice of a veteran Beamer.

High continued, "You'll see it time and again. It depends on the marketplace and revenue expectations. If Beamer as a company fails to reach the financial expectations, stockholders get mad."

These words in their exchange irritated me because for my Shittoon time I preferred quiet time. I considered throwing something over the barricades at them or chasing them out by using my toilet brush as a cutlass.

"But I don't understand. Why vendors?" asked Deep.

"Vendors are not Beamers. They are contracted employees. Like Jim and Patty, they are both vendors. They aren't Beamers."

Deep became confused, "What do you mean they aren't Beamers? We work with them everyday, they do the same thing as I do."

"Vendor contracts make us more flexible."

"But how can this constant fear of layoff help the business in the long term. Especially the stock price? What about Susan, on the last round of layoffs?"

No one cared about Susan in the Shittoon. Those yakkers were never so close to death as they were that moment, those gabbing nuisances standing and not stooling. They would walk the plank at brushpoint, gagged with one-ply stoolpaper.

High replied, "She was a vendor."

"But she worked hard. She scampered around doing all kinds of things. A heck of a lot more than myself, dare I say it. She'd been working here for twelve years. She told me herself. Who chooses who gets cut?"

"I don't know who chooses. I think the managers

collaborate on it. And of course they don't want to tell anyone who actually makes the choice, so no one knows who to shoot at, know what I mean? So no one goes Postal."

Deep said, "There should be some justification."

In the Shittoon, I crawled into the womb of a daydream and gave birth to a bull. The voices in the other half of the bathroom had ruined my sailing daydream, but another came to me. I imagined the life of a bull on a farm, or a Sire, as farmers call them. The creative energy of the Shittoon permeated my being.

Deep went on, "So that's why the people around the office have disappeared? I didn't ask until now."

Deep and High kept on talking, on and on, trying to interrupt my daydream, so I plugged my ears to concentrate. What a life the bull lived. The biggest risk in the bull's life passed in the first year of his life, when the farmer determined if the calf would remain a bull or become a steer. Male calves live a fine life for the first few months in the world. They eat well, their wobbly legs grow strong, and they even kick their heels in the air every once in awhile while practicing their moo. Then comes the day that male calves would never knowingly agree to; the day of neutering and sterility. One minute a male calf is eating his hay and drinking his water, and the next his testicles fall plumb to the dirty floor beneath them as the farmer moves on to the next calf. The calf bleats out due to the pain, but if the calf really knew the change of course his life had taken, his protest would be far greater. The farmer goes about the business of testicle removal in silence, perhaps even whistling a tune. It's all in a days work for the farmer.

However, a few male calves get to keep their maleness, but why only a few? In fact, why remove testicles in the first place?

To make them manageable, of course. To make them docile and more meaty. To make them profitable.

The calves that keep their maleness are destined for a different life. They will undergo certain hardships, like getting a huge ring pierced into their nose so the farmer can lead them around easier, but that fleeting pain is a small price when you consider the enormous amount of control the bull will wield over the herd. Imagine the excitement of a bull once he is loosed into a herd of docile cattle for the first time. On that day, he would begin his routine as usual: he'd munch on some hay in the morning (maybe a little feed), he'd drink some water, then maybe relax for a few hours in his pen. He may watch the cows through a crack in the barn and wonder why he yearns to be near them, knowing he wants to be near them. His nature makes him crave power, but only the farmer can fulfill his wish. Then the time comes when the farmer summons the bull for duty, and the bull instinctively tries to get away, but the farmer manages to coerce the bull's direction by slipping a rope through the nose-ring. The bull knew before the game started that the farmer would outwit him, and the bull curses himself as he runs into a waiting trailer the farmer has backed up to the pen. The trailer gate shuts the bull inside; the bull grows curious. Then the bull peers out of the thin slats in the wall of the trailer.

Soon the trailer is moving through the yard, to the main road. When the trailer wheels run over bumps in the road, the bull freezes up and bounces around, helplessly riding in near darkness. The bull wonders where the farmer has gone, growing worried, wishing the farmer were near for once. To the bull's relief, after a considerable drive, the trailer slows down and gradually stops, then backs up and stops again. The engine of the truck rumbles to a halt. In the silence, the bull expects something horrible to happen.

Soon the bull can hear the farmer talking, and realizes that all is well, feeling relief to know the farmer did not abandon him. The farmer talks to another man, who wears a flannel shirt and seed corn cap. The bull peeks out of the steel trailer slats and sees a new pasture, similar to the pasture he has oft watched cows graze in at the home farm, but not the same. Then the gate of the trailer jostles open, squeaking and grating as the steel handle turns and the hinges rotate.

Unaware of his own massive strength, the bull eases his way to end of the trailer and looks outside, acting like a child on the first day of school. Everything looks different in this new world. The farmer yells "Get on outta there! Hey-yah! Ssss!" and gives a good slap on the bull's hide. Startled, the bull leaps out of the trailer and trots several steps into the cow yard. With regained contempt, the bull eyes the farmer, who nonchalantly carries on his discussion with the other farmer. Both the bull and the farmer mistrust each other. So the bull strolls further into the cow yard, still watching the farmer with disgust. As the bull walks around, he sniffs the air. He rounds the silos and his field of vision opens wider, and he sees something he never thought he'd see. Around the silos, there in the distance grazes the prize he has yearned for - a herd of Holsteins.

The bull's heart rate increases. He looks for any obstacles between him and the herd. Is it possible? He starts walking, then galloping, then sprinting. Not a single obstacle. No fence. Not a gate. Nothing. Suddenly he knows what to do. The bull has been wanting this control for so long, yet he didn't know why.

The cows act afraid and run away. For the first time he's become the one in charge, so he chases them with zest and a new attitude. He can smell the air, and it doesn't matter who's first; he wants to meet with all of the cows. Like a cutting horse, the bull finds a fresh cow, and she's scared but still slows down for the inevitable mounting - she's been through this with other bulls before. The bull rears back, his front feet rise, and he climbs aboard to start his career as a sire, as the papa of many calves.

After the bull finishes with the first cow, he runs looking for another. Once he finds her, he mounts her without asking. He never asks again, either. Rather, he learns to take. He quickly learns which cows he will like, and which cows will get left alone.

All day he moves through the herd like a king through peasants. After a few hours, he has sired all he desires, and left the rest alone. Some of the cows follow the bull, to nuzzle and worship him, hoping to become his favorite cow, while other cows despise the bull for his arrogance and power over them.

The farmer suddenly returns, this time riding out to the pasture on a Suzuki four-wheeler. A newfound *cockiness* overtakes the bull, and he once again incorrectly judges that he can control the farmer. He rushes at the farmer, testicles aflap, running swiftly toward the four-wheeler, but the farmer shouts commands with force enough to scare the bull. The farmer deftly separates the bull from the cows, and before the bull knows it he is back in the trailer, furious at his compliance, furious at himself for allowing his capture, furious at the farmer for trumping his moment, wanting to kill the farmer and have all the power.

A knock rattled the Shittoon stall door. I was so surprised that I nearly deuced. The daydream died, and I realized that both of my legs had fallen asleep. Whoever was knocking would have to wait.

/* Concerning Danny's concerns about layoffs. */

When I finally returned to the office from the Shittoon, Danny immediately asked, "Did you hear anything about the layoffs?"

I said, "I heard something about a rumor. Vendors only or something."

"It had better be only the vendors," Danny whispered and shut the office door. "The word is out. Fillmore instant messaged me about it. This time it's for real. They are talking big layoffs, at the end of this week. And listen to this: the CEO is coming here to give a speech today. That is not good. Not good at all. Something is going down, perhaps the whole plant. Someday they will shut this whole Beamer site down. Right now I can't get laid off, I can't afford it."

For the rest of the day I heard buzzing in the hallways about potential layoffs. The CEO arrived with fanfare, and started to speak in the lunchroom. Hundreds of eager Beamers showed up for the CEO's speech. My chance of attending the massive meeting was null. Only people like my manager and Ted had invitations to see the CEO. But I watched the speech on the hallway monitors. The CEO's words sounded exactly like e-mails my manager sent me every day, full of Beamerspeak, except the CEO spoke with broad comments on the state of Beamer, and of America's economy, and of company goals and objectives. He reiterated his statements by reversing the sentence structures, over and over, hammering at the goals of Beamer. Whenever it seemed he had run out of ways to say the same thing a different way, he managed to find one more elaborate ordering of the same words. In the middle of the speech he announced that Beamer required a 'skills rebalancing.' Everyone watching the monitors took the news in silence. I did not catch on to the terminology. The CEO announced good news to our Minneapolis site, making his speech as upbeat as possible. After listening to the whole speech, I felt wonderful about the state of Beamer.

I went back to my debugging. Danny spent the afternoon overwrought with anguish over the CEO's speech.

I said, "That went pretty well, eh?"

Danny's face turned red. "Went well? That went like hell! I can't believe this."

I argued, "But the CEO said we are doing fine..."

Danny cut me off. "He said 'Skills Rebalancing.' Know what 'Skills Rebalancing' means? That's what he called it, Johnny. Starting today, I am looking for a new job, before he has a chance to lay me off."

The topic started to make me edgy as voices in the hallway filled the air with nervous thoughts and concerns over the CEO's speech.

Danny checked his e-mail, and became bitterly sarcastic.

"Holy Jesus, Mary, and Joseph. Johnny, listen to this, this is from some upper level management puke." Danny went on to read the note in a cartoon ogre voice: "It reads like this: 'Your management Team is aware that all Beamers are working hard, and we've decided to provide a low-cost little break for you and your co-workers to escape the daily grind for a while. What we've decided to do is have a party. March 22 is 'National Goof Off Day.' So from 11:00 to 12:00 on March 22 we are going to do exactly that: goof off! The management Team will bring dessert treats! Mmm...show up early! Your managers will be handing out your drink tickets to each of you. Each Beamer will receive two (2) tickets. In addition to drinks and dessert we'll have a few board games and puzzles to provide you the appropriate diversion to 'goof off' with. This is for Beamer employees only. Sorry, vendors are not invited. I'm looking forward to seeing you on March 22 for some Team building FUN!'"

Danny paused, then mocked, "Oh, wow, a party, huh Johnny? I'm sure they'll buy us the cheapest cake they can find, too. This is all a diversion for what's really about to go down."

Danny shook his peanut head in disbelief.

Shortly after the Goof Off day party ended, a man across the hall received his layoff notice. I had never talked to him before. A few people stopped by to say goodbye to the man and offer condolences. Soon he disappeared from the office, and the next day a new body filled his adjustable chair. Fillmore, Danny, and I had no idea who the new guy was. We didn't know if he was working in our department or planting a bomb. I said hello to the man one day, but he only looked at me and turned away, so I never bothered him again.

That week of pandemonium ended to my relief, and even more of a relief to Danny. The entire event weighed on my psyche like a corpse, and my chest felt tight as a snare drum.

* * * * *

I intended to call you that night, Katya, but was distracted. With the next section of memoirs, I expect that I may offend you greatly, so I make ample apologies in advance. But in order to be entirely honest with you, by necessity these words must be included as part of the significant Beamer Nights.

/* How Jamie fared at Beamer, and how the neighborhood became very friendly to my baser appetites. */

That weekend, Jamie spent his time playing a video game online against some of his devout friends. Jamie's character walked through the game wielding a hand-cannon as he murdered every zombie, alien, and fiend in his path. Jamie admitted that the appeal of cutthroat combat overruled his disgust for violence. I asked him how work was treating him.

He shrugged, "Not bad. I've been...Oh, there he is! I knew he was in this sector! Now I'm going to roll up behind him....and waste him from his weak side. Work?...I've been busy. I've actually been working with customers, doing the role of a consultant right now."

"Really?" I said. "I thought you were doing the system administrator thing?"

"Watch this, Johnny. He doesn't know I'm behind him right now. I'm loading up the big gun right now...oh yeah, that's right, that's me barkin' fire! Wooo!"

Jamie launched a phosphorous grenade into the chest of his opponent. When the grenade detonated, the opposing character's armor and flesh burned white hot in an agonizing death. The instant cremation of the character showed his heart fall out of his chest and continue to beat on the ground for a few seconds before Jamie's character came up and knifed the heart five or six times.

Jamie said, "And that's all she wrote for him! Man, that never gets old...sorry, Johnny. Back to your question: I'll be setting up the product on customer systems. I'm basically acting as a sales engineer, or a sales consultant. Kind of cool, I guess. It still sucks."

I said, "A sales engineer slash consultant. Sounds like a good title. Are you going to start traveling out of town?"

"I think they are going to make me a local rep to go out to customer sites in the metro area. But get this: Last week these customers, a real bunch of jerks, one guy in particular, wouldn't stop calling us for help. He said they tried to get the Beamer software up and running themselves but failed. So my manager sent me out and told me to take a look. I couldn't believe the mess. They had mangled some files and needed a simple reinstall. It was a mess, to say the least. Then I started modifying things, monkeying with this and that. And this one guy, this vulture, hung over my shoulder the whole time. But after a few hours I told him that I was returning to the Beamer site and I'd log on to their system from my office. The guy looked like he was going to cry. He tried to make a scene, but I left."

I asked, "So you got everything working for the customer?"

"Heck yes," Jamie laughed, "there wasn't much to it really. I logged onto the customer's system from my office and finished the job. But because the guy irritated me so darn much, I remained logged on that day and the next day. I charged them for fifteen hours of work, when it was really only about three hours."

"You're kidding? Can't they find out?"

"How would they know? They are as clueless as the day is long. Besides, other guys in the department do stuff like that all the time. That's how our department makes money. We charge X amount of dollars per hour, so we try to get as many hours as possible for each job. Believe me, an hour of consulting is not cheap either."

"Wow," I said, "I would never have guessed such a thing is legal."

"Legal or not, it's business. Time for the next game. This guy I'm playing against is getting addicted to this game. I've been addicted to this game for years. Probably be a late night for me. I gotta slaughter this dude a few more times, then I have to go to Bible Study."

"Have fun, Jamie," I said. "I'm going to go buy some ice cream."

"Oh, Johnny wait," Jamie said, "I almost forgot to tell you - make sure to lock the doors on the garage. This homeless guy has moved into the neighborhood. He slinks around to each of the trash bins outside of the houses. I talked to a lady down the street about it, and I think she's going to notify the police of the situation. He shouldn't be in this neighborhood."

"Thanks for the warning. I think I saw that man in the park one day. The poor guy."

"Yes, well, the poor guy can go terrorize some other neighborhood," Jamie protested.

When I stepped outside, I looked across the street at Shawna's house. She was standing in the window gazing out with a sad face. She noticed me and then smiled and waved before coming out the front door. She walked across the street up my driveway, smiling from head to toes, making me amorous for her.

"Well, I was sure hoping to run into you one of these days," Shawna said. "Sometimes neighbors around here are just not very welcoming, are they?"

I smiled as my sinful eyes focused on Shawna's breasts.

She went on, "And you haven't had the tour of my house yet, have you?"

I said, "It's true, I haven't been inside. What about the man you live with? Your husband?"

"Now, now, that's ex-husband, Johnny. He's off fishing or doing God-knows-what. Let me assure you, he and I are a thing of the past, Johnny. Let me *assure* you of that."

I pointed to her hand, "Then why do you still wear the diamond ring?"

She blushed, "I don't know. I just like it. It was expensive, that's why."

A diamond is a girl's best friend, I reasoned.

She smiled, "Well, come on then. Come take the tour."

I stuttered, "I was going to get some ice cream at the store."

"I have a whole pail of ice cream. I'll even make you a bowl."

"What kind is it?"

"Neopolitan." She teased me with her eyes by widening them.

"Believe it or not, that's my favorite," I said.

My feet led me into her house. She turned on the TV and she showed me the kitchen, she showed me the living room, the dining room, the basement, the wash room, and the bedrooms. She bumped into me several times during the tour, pressing her taut shirt against my arm, gathering all my undue attention. At the end of the tour, she told me to sit down on the couch, so I sat quietly. A dog came up to me, put his head in my crotch and gazed at me. I asked the dog to leave, but the dog preferred to stay. Shawna called the dog away and locked him in a bedroom.

Compared to her usual garb she was dressed-down. She wore a designer pair of jeans and a tank top. Her breasts filled the shirt well, and the jeans showed her marvelous curvature that begged for touching. She returned to the living room, sat down on the couch near me, and made small talk. After a few minutes of averting my eyes from hers, she stopped talking. I felt her eyes on me, waiting for me to look at her again. She moved closer to me. I turned; she locked onto my eyes. Then she kissed me. And her arms circled my neck. My past experiences with younger and less attractive women made me a fumbling wreck with Shawna, as I was overcome by desire. My chest loosened from the stress of the Beamer week. A thought of Katya entered my mind, but all rational thought left me as the couch became the scratching post for desire. Shawna undressed in front of me, without inhibition, and I felt like Moses at the parting of her thighs as she freed the oppressed inside me. What a night it turned out to be. She brought her knees up on the couch, I tickled, she giggled, I pressed, she reached, I pushed, she pulled my hair, I yanked hers, she punched me. She crawled onto the floor away from me, I crawled after. In the bedroom we continued, on the bed, hanging off the bed, falling to the floor. I could see in her face how desperate she was; the poor thing was an exile of love. Surely, I had the same look due to my prolonged involuntary abstinence. I guessed that she wanted me to be her new boyfriend from then on.

Afterward, I took a cigarette from her pack of Camels, and decided that I was supposed to smoke after casual intercourse based on various movies I had watched.

"So you are quite a cowboy," Shawna said.

"That's right, but very scrawny," I joked.

"Yes, you are," she laughed. "I really shouldn't let you smoke in here. My ex would kill me."

"When is he moving out of here?"

"Soon."

I questioned her life as the night wore on. I asked about the ex-husband, where he was moving, what he was like.

She said, "He's a jerk. I hate him, the lousy bastard."

She said, "I don't know where he'll slum off to when he moves."

She said, "He's a psycho. See the front door? He nearly tore it off one night. He's an ex-Marine. He was on active duty for eight years."

Oh wonderful, I thought. I'm a weak-backed Beamer and the ex-husband could twist my neck like a bottlecap.

The more I asked questions of her, the less cohesive her answers became. Her face turned sad. She downplayed my questions and kissed my neck, or instead of answering she just rolled my over and teased me. I pressed on with the questions, until she stopped answering and flopped to her side on the bed, turning her head away from me. She bit at her nails and became rife with sadness.

"I lied to you," she whimpered.

"About what?"

"I'm so sorry. I am such a bad person…I lied to you…"

She sobbed and sobbed. I comforted her by saying, "I'm

sure you aren't as bad as you say. You seem a wonderful person, full of passion. I feel lucky to have met such a beautiful, single woman. What's bothering you?"

"I'm still married," she cried.

"Holy jumping-Jesus!" I exclaimed, "You said it was over with."

"I don't know what it is anymore...with him," she sobbed.

Suddenly the evening changed; the air grew heavy; my mood atrophied. Her tears made my shoulder wet and caused makeup to diffuse on her face. Listening to her story I felt sympathy because the husband treated her so poorly. Continually she disclosed stories of the husband's infidelity and imprudence.

"He's always out drinking, or running around," she said, "and I find phone numbers written in women's handwriting in his wallet. I am done with him, Johnny. Seriously. You have to believe me. Just last week I picked up the phone and someone on the other end hung up right away. Please don't hate me, Johnny."

"I don't hate you, I feel sorry for you, being treated so badly and all."

She begged, "Please stay with me tonight."

A crossroads waited in front of me to pick a direction. I could leave or stay for dessert. Well, her beauty struck me dumb. Leaving was incongruous with my desire. Then Shawna made my decision for me by performing the most amorous kind of encouragement. The attitude of the whole evening allowed me to forget about work; she shook the bugs out of me, in a sense. I thought of Katya again, but quickly let her pass out of my mind to avoid any guilt, even though she and I were not dating. I looked out of the bedroom window and saw a squirrel, bobbing his head, laughing at our nudeness. Shawna threw a pillow at the window and the squirrel disappeared.

"That's the same squirrel from the birdbath," Shawna said. "He's a nuisance."

Shawna and I spent the rest of the night enjoying one another's company as many times as possible. The dog stayed locked in the room all night.

I woke up that night in her marital bed, suddenly fearful that the husband might be coming home. While she slept, I frantically collected my clothes. She looked sad as she slept, with her makeup smeared down her cheeks from crying. I crept out the front door and crossed the street to my house, wondering if I had committed adultery or just Shawna had, or if both of us had. The following day I kept thinking to myself, "I need to call Katya," but I fretted all day about a crazed husband coming to find me and string me up in the yard like a trophy deer. I did not call Katya. The husband never came looking for me. And after that night, Shawna did not come looking for me either.

/* An epiphany regarding Fillmore, and how I became a Cleverton. */

After such a lusty Beamer night, I couldn't wait to return to work. That Monday, I arrived at 4:00 AM, obsessed with the thought of the husband tracking me down and slaughtering me. I found myself looking at the code and imagining scenarios regarding of my death. I accomplished nothing, and almost felt relieved when Danny arrived at 10:00. Right on schedule, Fillmore came trotting down to the office to meet Danny for morning prattle.

Since the first time Fillmore cudgeled her way into the office to talk to Danny, I felt that I'd seen her before, somewhere in the annals of my life. She had a familiar long face.

"Oops! Sorry, Johnny," she said as her rear displaced my head.

As she turned her body sideways to park herself, a realization came to me. Finally I knew what had been bothering me about Fillmore, and it was this: she resembled a horse. After noticing her body carriage and structure, I had a hard time stifling laughter when I looked at her mouth and waited for her to whinny. I half expected her to nuzzle my arm and look at me dreamily, hoping that I might have a carrot. Her backside, the same backside that bumped my head on a daily basis, seemed a rump. She tied her hair back like a blonde mane that flowed at her neck. I couldn't help wondering if she occupied a stable at night, or if she kept sugar cubes in her office, or if she gallivanted when out of the Beamers' sight at the end of the work day.

How childish and rude it was to think in this manner, but she wore flip-flop shoes that clip-clopped in the hallway so that I knew when she was nearing. And each time she'd leave my office, she'd clip-clop in her flip-flops back to her office, or ranch, perhaps.

All week, during Fillmore's time spent in my office, I listened to Danny and her complain with pleasure, drowning out my imagination. Whenever I turned to debugging, my mind receded into a shell of wanton fear of Shawna's husband. By Friday, I had reclaimed a feeling of general security, but still struggled to concentrate. I admonished myself to no avail, finding the long periods of stagnant debugging disheartening. In fact, from that week onward, the art of debugging became drudgery to my instincts as a programmer. How I had ever considered debugging enjoyable escaped me.

The entire day felt like a trial-and-error as I stepped through the vast sea of code. Where had my patience gone off to? How could I complain while making such ample wages? How could anyone complain when his bank account was bursting with cash? Even the comfort of the Shittoon did not jumpstart the occasion for effective debugging.

The entire week, I fixed no bugs at all, which soon become the norm. Over nearly a month's time I fixed two bugs, far beneath my original expectations. And over the next few months I became less and less productive because I became a *Cleverton*.

One day, the Korean fellow across the hall again started to instant-message me. I quickly became accustomed to spending an entire afternoon deep in clever conversations. Thousands of words darted through the sockets between our two computers. The internet had spawned a whole new species of *Clevertons*. The Korean fellow and I spent days and weeks making up personal cartoons, inside jokes, and esoteric languages that allowed us to pass the time. The instant messaging outlet became the only creative fixation for us, supplanting our will to debug with useless witticisms. Oftentimes I had several chats going at once, with other Beamers that the Korean fellow introduced me to. All of the Korean fellows friends were flamboyant on the instant messenger; happy people that seemed to enjoy my company online. Together we played trivia games, crosswords, wrote mini-scripts for mock TV shows, and discussed movies. To give an example of my development as a *Cleverton*, I created *The Adventures of Sue Pasta and Joe Ravioli*. The Korean fellow and I spent at least a week chatting and dreaming about the characters. This was the story:

"Sue Pasta and Joe Ravioli came to life after Don Barilla, AKA 'The Fork' went overboard one day with habanero sauce. The noodle dish he prepared was a mixture of sundry Italian noodles. He cooked fanatically and spasmodically in a cauldron like the witches of *Macbeth*, bubbling the cauldron over with jalapeno, habanero, Tobasco, pepperoncinis, and even a pinch or two of smokeless tobacco. During the course of this inferno, a single ravioli, Joe Ravioli, and a single lasagna noodle, Sue Pasta, sprung to life and slid off the countertop to escape Don Barilla. When Don Barilla chased the two supernoodles, they discovered they had certain powers riven into them by the excessive use of habanero. Don Barilla struggled to capture them because he felt these noodles were the spiciest of all, but through a series of cute superhero moves, the noodles escaped 'The Fork.' Joe Ravioli has the ability to bounce on his belly. Sue Pasta can shape her body into a rope, or a spitwad-shooter, or a dart. Together the noodles forever run away from Don Barilla, with romantic tension between them that never reaches fruition. Shy Joe Ravioli always blushes, and brash Sue Pasta attempts to hide her attraction to chubby Joe...et cetera."

The discussions went on and on. There were 'side-dish' characters like Vermin Celli and Musty Celli, who played Don Barilla's thugs and foiled most of his genius plans through their own bumbling. There were the Tiny Parmesans and, well, frankly, much more of this sort of crap. The Korean fellow and I even wrote five episodes in script format over the instant messenger, foolishly believing a cartoon publisher would latch onto the idea. By the following Monday we became bored with the idea of Sue Pasta and Joe Ravioli entirely. Suddenly the whole thing died, and we moved on to the next clever idea. The focus of a *Cleverton* is fickle.

I had been working at Beamer for one year. How the boredom of debugging had gripped me in a matter of one year concerned me. I worried about growing incompetent. Although I had become quite efficient and useful at debugging, I now glozed over the code missing important bits of information.

I prompted myself with the harrowing introspection, "Am I becoming apathetic because I'm incompetent, or becoming incompetent because I'm apathetic?"

/* What the manager thought of my behavior, and Ted's project for me, thanks to an Asian-Irishwoman. */

My manager reviewed my recent performance in a different light than I did. He held a weekly scheduled meeting with me, a one-on-one meeting, to discuss my state of Beamerhood. These meetings marked the only time the manager and I ever saw one another, because his schedule of meetings with various groups and individuals consumed all of his waking hours.

Each week, he first took out a piece of paper to record the minutes of our meeting. He said, "Johnny, how are you doing? Sit down, have a seat, tell me about yourself. How are things?"

"Whir."

Using standard Beamerspeak, I rambled on about the nature of the bug I was working on, such as, "...The latest bug involves a Portuguese system running the previous version of Beamer WebCutter. The dates get garbled when our code passes in the English word 'Today' and the localized Portuguese software can't recognize the word because the Portuguese word for today is 'Hoje,' however it's actually pronounced. I suspect this fails on all Beamer WebCutters running in languages other than English, so I need to provide a fix that recognizes the problem for all locales."

With his head tilted, my manager said, "Great. That's great, Johnny. That sure sounds like a good bug to fix. Anything else?"

"Whir."

"Yes there is another bug I'm working on," I smiled, "These guys in Virginia somewhere are running a remote application that connects to our WebCutter via HTTP, and somewhere along the line it fails on a communication failure exception, with a minor code of 6."

He scribbled notes on his paper while I spoke. For three weeks straight I told my manager the same story of the same two bugs, almost verbatim, and he nodded and scribbled his notes, oblivious to the redundancy of my lies. The third time I told the same story, he interrupted me with a look of concern on his face.

He paused and tapped his pencil on the desk. He increased the lilt of his voice.

"Now, I know you work alone, Johnny. You basically are your own Team, and I know that not a lot of opportunities come up to meet Team members, but it's important to meet and work with others. We are trying to stress the importance of 'Team' right now at Beamer. I have to pass this information along to you, because our department is only as strong as our bonds at work. You know what they say - a chain is only as strong as its weakest link. We have a lot of hard working people here. Shut the door, will you, please, Johnny?"

I closed the door reluctantly, expecting to be fired in the whir.

"Every year we do a ranking of each employee to determine his or her annual raise and/or bonus. Usually the newest department employees receive a mediocre rating. You know, somewhere in the middle of the road. But Johnny, I have no choice but to evaluate your work differently."

Bracing myself to cry, I sat rigidly in the chair, thinking of how to commence groveling to keep my job, and how to make up for time spent as a *Cleverton*.

The manager continued, "Beamer gives ratings from 1 to 5, with five being given to employees of outstanding merit and one meaning...well...meaning room for improvement. Because of your solutions on some of the bugs, I'm going to give you the highest rating of the whole department. And I actually have a sheet here stating this in writing. You see here...the percent of your raise will be twenty-five percent. Not bad for a year of work, eh? And if you look here, you'll see your salary will increase this much."

My eyes grew big at the number.

He continued, "This is Beamer's way of saying 'keep up the good work.' We'll reward you if you work hard, and I've seen nothing but hard work from you. But remember, the Team is the focus, and if I can get more members of the Team to work like you, well, we will have productivity like we have never seen before. The Team is really starting to gel and work as a team. We all help each other, like geese flying in a V, or bricks holding up an arch. Know what I mean?"

I wiped my dewy eyes and beamed at my manager. "Yes. Thank you. I will try to measure up to your generosity."

He said, "Also, Johnny. You are supposed to go talk to Ted. He has something for you to work on."

"Gladly."

"One last thing, Johnny - how bout them Green Bay Packers?"

As I left the manager's office, a guilty abstraction of my soul lumped in my throat. I scurried to Ted's office to ask him what he needed, whatever it was; I would have skydived without a parachute at that moment if the company asked me to.

Ted greeted me in his office, waving me in while he

dialed on his phone. He initiated a conference call as I sat down quietly.

"Hello? Hello?" Ted said, "Anybody in Ireland today?" He waited a bit before saying to me, "Well, they must be running late. But that gives me a chance to talk to you..."

"Hallo? Hallo? Dis es Sue Xiong-O'Flaherty calleeng fum Dublin..." A voice came across the line with a strong Asian-Irish accent.

Ted broke away from me to speak to the phone. "Yes, I'm here. This is Ted. Is everybody in place now?"

The voice said, "Yas. Eveebody es hee-ah. We still aw missing a few, but dey chood be wit us chotly. I hop."

Ted said, "Let's get started anyway. For those of you who don't know me I'm Ted Jablonski, chief architect of the WebCutter product here in Minnesota. I'm sitting here with Johnny Pepper, the software engineer who will be working on this transition project. Johnny, why don't you say hello?"

Stunned, I sat wondering what project I could possibly be working on.

The voice said, "Hallo? Ah you still deyah?"

Ted said, "Yes, we're still here. I accidentally hit the mute button on the keypad, sorry about that. Go on, Johnny. You were saying?"

"Well, I debug," I stalled, "I'm a debugger. I debug...stuff."

Ted assisted me, "Johnny's one of our best developers on the server side."

A rush of blood filled my face. Ted winked at me and

spoke fluidly to the Asian-Irishwoman. I tried to listen carefully but could not understand what Ted referred to. Also, I had difficulty understanding the Asian-Irishwoman because her accent was like nothing I had ever heard before.

In a five minute monologue, Ted described the design of the project he expected me to work on. Whether or not I truly understood anything didn't matter to Ted; he went right ahead and asked me if I could give an estimated timeline for project completion.

"What do you think, Johnny? Can we finish this project in four months?" Ted gave me a thumbs-up and winked. He pushed mute on the phone and said to me, "Say five months, Johnny." Then he un-muted the phone.

I said, "Well, I don't know. I think five months might be more like it for a project of this scope."

Ted laughed silently, and then said to the phone, "Yeah, I'm sorry Sue; this type of thing might take a while. All of our other developers have full plates right now."

Sue said, "Dat's too long time fame. We ot least need wooking prototype befoah dat."

"Well, this is a little late in the cycle to be adding product requirements," Ted said. "But we will see what we can do."

The voice said, "Johnny, if you hoff queschuns, pease caw us fo hep."

Ted concluded the conversation and hung up.

Ted asked, "Never been in a conference call before, Johnny?"

"No."

"Well, you have been now. Did you understand what we were talking about?"

I said, "Not really. Not at all, actually."

"Here's the deal," Ted said. "This Beamer department in Ireland wants us to build a set of plug-ins for WebCutter so that other Beamer products can have access to our web functionality. But they've requested this feature too late to make it in the next release of WebCutter. Had they requested it six months ago, or a year ago, we could have added it to this release. Now we only have about six months to get the plug-ins coded, not to mention we didn't budget for this labor. I thought this could be the perfect project for you to work on, along with your debugging. Or is the debugging keeping you busy enough already?"

"Oh, I'm not that busy...I mean...I'm busy with the bugs, and happy with them, but a project sounds more exciting than debugging. Not that I hate debugging, I just..."

Ted stopped me, "I know what you mean. Debugging gets old fast. Ok, then. You are assigned to this project. You have to try and finish a prototype within five months. That's why I had you say five months on the phone - to buy you some extra time. The nice thing about conference calls is the invisibility on either end."

I smiled at Ted's knowledge of everything.

Ted laughed, "Let's go get some coffee while I tell you all about this project. But a word of warning - this will require you to spend a lot of time at work, including weekends and evenings."

"That's terrific," I said.

"Johnny, I think that's the first time I've ever heard anyone get excited about working nights and weekends."

/* How I called the beautiful Katya, reestablishing diplomacy between us. */

The anticipation of the project excited me immensely. It excited me so much, that I called you, Katya, that same night. Excitement spilled over the phone line as I said,

"Katya, I'm sorry for walking out on you at the restaurant that night so long ago. Can I make it up to you in someway, someday?"

But you had a boyfriend at that time, Katya. You said, "It's too late, Johnny Pepper."

So instead I sent flowers with a tiny love letter penned for you that read.

"Forever in arrears am I for she

Who thieves all thoughts and stole my heart."

I planned to snuff out your boyfriend with pollen. I instructed the florist to send the same flowers every Friday following that week.

Pete Flies

/* How I spent five months in a Beamer hermit container. */

Finally - actual engineering to apply to my title of Software Engineer. I laid code down like a cement truck in the coming months, paving the black world with green text. I tweaked the Asian-Irishwoman's whitepaper design, I guttered the needless levels of inheritance and rewrote hideous templates into manageable polymorphic abstracts, carefully allocating memory off the heap, growing my arrays with prudence, writing appropriate deconstructors where garbage collection was questionable to avoid leaks that could lead me toward segmentation faults, and I directed my pointers in the hash table to give me a Big-O(n) lookup times for remote clients using a unique address as the hash value, using a multithreaded broker to handle requests with pseudo-event driven routines spurred by queued buffers, calling functions across programming languages using native specs so I could pass in wads of data to be reassembled on the other side...allowing for remote apps to call my new API directly with no extra socket creation. I used exception handlers that overrided standard I/O to use a secure log file...and groped through GUI manuals to find appropriate layouts in devising an interface in accord with the Beamer preferred look and feel.

The project stretched my work hours right past the sun into Beamer nights, though I had no idea since I just stayed indoors slapping away at my keyboard. Often I did not leave my hermit container at all, even at night, except to get more Mountain Dew and Nutty Bars. When I did go home, I stayed plugged in to the project.

The project became an exercise in total containment. When the first line of code compiled, the office transformed into a hermit container; a voluntary prison to be used for Object Oriented programming, in which every programmable construct contained something or was contained by something else, containment.

Programming models reflect the world itself, with certain conceptual abstractions. To represent a physical object with a programming language requires an examination of the physical object. Take a shoe, for instance. What does a shoe do? What properties does the shoe have? What is the ultimate purpose of a shoe? - The purpose is to contain a foot. Not just any foot, but a human foot with a specific size and shape.

Anything containable or contained is programmable.

My office itself was a container of things. The office contained the desk, which contained the computer, which contained the circuits, which contained the electrical bits. The office was contained by the floor (level 3). The floor contained by the building (building 35). The building contained by the Beamer site. The site by the city. The city by the county. The county by the state. State by country. Country, continent, world, solar system, galaxy, universe. Containment.

Quark, neutron, nucleus, atom, organelle, cell, tissue, organ, system, body.

I became rather smitten with the theory of Containment.

* * * * *

The general rule of the theory of Containment is that everything real is contained. All matter is contained in four dimensions: x, y, z, and time. Computers can break the rules of dimension, but not physically. Not really. Computers cannot break the rules of Containment. Again, everything real is contained. Humans can only think in terms of Containment and breaking the rules means impossibility. I reduced the physical

Universe to only three categories: containers, adhesives, and items.

One day, after making much progress on the project, after I had imbibed a large volume of Mountain Dew, I commenced writing certain rules of Containment on the white board in my office. When Danny arrived at his usual hour of 10:00 in the morning, he immediately started to read what I had written:

He read, "'A finite universe allows Containment. Without a finite maximum container we have chaos; we cannot exist. Infinity disallows any Containment; unlimited space allows nothing to stay together. Without a finite space, containers cannot interact. The limits of the universe allow containers within to interact.' What the hell is that?" Danny whined, "A new paradigm or something?"

I paused in my writing. I said, "Danny, you ever heard of a theory of Containment?"

"No." He sniffed at the air. "Johnny, when was the last time you shaved? Or bathed?"

"Never mind then, Danny." I sat down and continued working on the project, but kept thinking, *containment*.

I held out my finger in front of my nose, followed it with my eye, making my finger the cause for my eye movement. The finger moves the eye, in a sense, as an example of Containers interacting. Actions cause containers to interact. The action of speaking causes the Danny container to respond. Rather, speech causes many different containers to move. For example, upon speech, the Danny container turns toward me, then his eyeballs, then his lung containers breath rancid air on my neck. That is the initial series of changes caused by my speech in the office.

Maybe that's too in depth, I thought. Taking a top view

of the situation, I looked at the universe first. Notice that the universe is the ultimate container, silent and awesome. The wall of the universe is the maximum container; the limit, or frame. The wall. The blocker. Yes, the wall might expand and contract, but no matter what, the limit exists, whether we are in the primordial soup, a Big-Bang daze, or where we are today.

The universe contains all items, but the major ones are galaxies, stars, and solar systems. If we can take the largest universe item, a galaxy, and study it briefly, we find that the adhesive of a galaxy is gravity, and that the items of the galaxy are stars and planets.

With that in mind Containment breaks down further into a solar system. In the solar system container we also have gravity as adhesive, and here planets and stars are items. Now take a planet. A planet is a container with a gravity adhesive as well, among other things, like ferrous liquids cooled into solid glue. Our planet has cooled enough that we have various adhesives within and without, so that if the solar system disbanded somehow, the Earth container would stay together based on its adhesive core. Of course, the humans would all die terrible deaths, but that's not really the point.

What items are Contained by the Earth?

Myself. And Danny. We are items in the same container, which is sickening to consider. What else? There are computers, trees, air masses, and billboards. There are cigarettes, hillbillies, infomercials, cupboards, hustlers, hoo-hoos, tallywackers, and talismans. There's more.

Little things represent containment better yet. The project I worked on, for example, contained very small flits of electricity in the allocation of magneto-electrical memory into terabyte, gigabyte, megabyte, kilobyte, byte, bit...

The computer awaited my instruction as I pondered Containment. I wrote a few more lines of code, pulled at my mop of hair, and started to compile the project. A piece of hair fell from my head to my desktop.

Then I went on with the theory: consider the Containment in a single strand of hair. The keys to the universe and knowledge of all things exist in one strand of hair. In a string of hair are cells, each cell with its own little frame, and its own little adhesive. All cells have walls. They bond to certain other things. Each cell is a container...with many, many wonderful items inside, but on the same principal of Containment, each mitochondria or ribosome contains itself - each little organelle contains its very own items. Tiny, tiny containers!

The atom, the electron, the neutron are the lower limits of Containment...

Danny complained, "Quit bouncing your legs. You are shaking my desk."

The bricks of Containment theory are atoms, the littlest of items. The atom is the tiniest container, and the universe the biggest. Is it possible that something smaller exists? For sure. Is it possible that our universe resides inside another container, a container that holds many universes, or just our universe and something else, maybe a large bassoon? Absolutely. But humans may never know. Perhaps we are not able to know the outliers of Containment theory. As humans, we are like cells in the roots of a tree that are only able to comprehend the tree and no more. Humans cannot really know anything outside of the maximum container. That's why everything humans build or program into computers is built using the theory of Containment; because that's all we know. We only emulate Containment, and cannot think beyond it.

What about ideas?

Imaginary. Ideas are total constructs of electrical activity inside human containers. Imagination is uncontainable, therefore not real. Of course, humans find this anomaly of imagination fascinating due to its intrinsic property of *uncontainment*. Most human pursuits in art and science allege to contain uncontainable imaginations; Literature, science, linguistics, religion, philosophy all try to nail down uncontainable properties. Claims have been set forth to seize victory over these imaginations, but few have succeeded. Perhaps only science has contained any imaginations, such as explaining the eclipses, the solar system, the four seasons, and the nature of germs and disease. But these discoveries of humans have only shown containers to be where we could previously see no container. Many people do not wish to hear new rules of Containment, and therefore take hundreds of years to accept new proofs of Containment. The Catholic Church did not pardon Galileo until the late twentieth century for exposing his Containment facts. Containment scares people if too factual or deprecating to their imaginations.

Try to contain love, thought, truth, emotion, or faith. Or a theme. These things are not real. The second rule of Containment theory is, imagination cannot be contained, and therefore imaginary ideas are not real.

The computer stopped computing, and printed:

Syntax error: line 2135, BrokerRegistry.c - Scope resolution operator missing.

I fixed the code error at line 2135 and recompiled. I picked up a Beamer WebCutter manual that had been sitting on my desk.

This book, I thought, holding the book in my hand. Look at this book. Opening the book, it contains pages, and the adhesive for the book is the binding. Each page is also a container, holding words. But words are parts of sentences that have punctuation as adhesives. Words are items in the sentence structures. Words without order are useless.

But what if I don't want to read this book? And say I am an animal, perhaps a town squirrel. This book's pages are about as useful to me as a kitchen blender. So what would I do as a squirrel with this container? Step on it, perhaps, to elevate my height. I might chew on it for fun, to sharpen my teeth items. In essence, containers that are entirely useful to one group are useless to another group.

Money, too. The imaginary value of money is shown by how a currency revered in one nation might be thrown out as rubbish in another. What is a precious stone in one locale, might be gravel elsewhere. Value cannot be contained outside the confines of the mind.

The computer stopped computing and printed:

Syntax error: line 2135, BrokerRegistry.c - Scope resolution operator missing.

The monitor displayed an error, indicating I failed to fix the compile error, causing me to react and fix the same syntax error on the same line as before. I forgot to save my changes. Causing me to cuss under my breath. Anger.

Anger is imaginary. Not real. Yet imagination can affect objects. Serial killers imaginations affect many containers.

If I were angry, I might tear the pages out of this book, indirectly changing the Containment of the book.

"That's my book!" Danny yelped.

* * * * *

There, the pages are strewn about the office and I can see the book itself no longer has Containment of pages. I hold an empty binding. Not much of a container anymore. More like an item now, perfectly useless to me. The pages still contain the sentences on the floor, but the book lacks its whole definition. However, now the squirrel would definitely prefer this version of the book, as stuffing for his winter nest.

"The manager will hear about this," Danny said, "You had better order another WebCutter book for me!"

The office: a Beamer container. The building, the halls, the vending machines, the sinks, the computer monitors, the arrays, the pointers inside the computer...the graphical user interfaces acting as containers on the PC screen; even abstract concepts are presented as containers. Humans cannot build anything without a container in mind. Even the most abstract art is contained; artists cannot break free of Containment, though they fancy they can.

"You had better apologize to...hey, look at me," Danny commanded.

A sound wave is a container, too, with the wavelengths as the items. Tighten the wavelengths up or spread them apart, you still have Containment. Waves of light and sound are like sentences in air and space. Atrophy and entropy only matter subjectively, in the eye of the beholder; the idea of Containment itself is subjective. If the sun went dry of all light and the living things on planet earth died, all containers that we as humans know would die and atrophy, but only in our human opinion. To the rest of the universe, the energy would simply have moved on to somewhere else, to a different level of Containment.

"God dammit, answer me," said Danny bitterly.

God? If someone can observe and define a larger container than the universe, so be it. Containment theory will still hold true. Until then, it is imagination. Something uncontained? Is God to be described as a containable item or uncontainable? The question to be asked any object is, "Could I put it in a box? Or program a representation of it?"

What is an item uncontained? This very question may be the crux of the meaning of life, I concluded.

Danny said, "That's it, I'm going to get some coffee. I need to take a walk. This is too much for me."

When Danny left, the project finished compiling, finally without any syntax errors. The code worked when I ran it. The project was complete at long last.

I looked at the calendar on my computer. Five months had passed. Five months?

Five months of life, fast as a cursor blink.

/* How the unexpected reaction from Ted spurred me to be a boorish ass. */

I told Ted that everything fit the schedule, my code needed only a few finishing touches and I was done.

Ted frowned.

"Listen, Johnny. Sit down," he said, "I just got out of a meeting with the department managers and the architect in Ireland. It seems...we are not going to need your code now."

"What?" I said aggressively, "Are you joking, Ted? Just last week the Asian-Irishwoman e-mailed me asking how progress went."

"I know. I know. I'll tell you why," Ted exhaled. "We've decided to stick with our old way of doing things for the next release of WebCutter, to avoid any maintenance of new code. The marketplace is too volatile right now with so many new technologies coming out, and rather than pigeonhole ourselves with our version, we feel that waiting for an industry standard to emerge is the right thing to do."

"But I can adapt the code to the standard," I pleaded.

Ted put his hand on my shoulder. "I have no doubt. But this decision comes down the chute from Ireland. That's the way they want to handle it. They want to buy someone else's software to do the same things you've programmed, and the reason for this is maintenance on the code. That way Beamer will not have to maintain or debug your code."

"Why did you wait to tell me about it? I worked on this for five months. Everything works great...What a waste of

Beamer money..."

"I know, I know. It sucks. I've been through it myself, more than you want to know. Beamer can be like the military sometimes - 'hurry up and wait' they say. Or 'attack that hill' then they tell you to retreat once you've conquered it. But hang on to the code you wrote for the project. Keep it in case we change our mind. Beamers in Ireland made the decision on this one, so don't think I made you work a pointless project. I'm just the bearer of bad news. Don't worry about it. Go home for the day. Oh! And before I forget, great job on this project, Johnny. Even if it won't be used for anything. You have no reason to feel bad about it."

Slowly, like an unshaved zombie, I moped out of Ted's door. My container became immediately depressed. Back in my office, I put on my jacket and left for the day, even though noon was yet an hour away.

Danny said, "Where are you going so soon? Abusing the rules, are you?"

I said, "Eat me, Danny."

Danny's smug face turned sour. ".What did you say to me? You better watch yourself, Johnny. I'll take this straight to the manager."

I didn't answer; I allowed him to speak.

"Let me tell you," the dimple in Danny's chin warbled, "let me inform you of something: I know karate." He put up his spindly arms and made little wads of fists that looked like bread dough.

I said, "You couldn't karate out of a wet paper bag, you smelly puffer," knowing that neither could I for that matter. I left the office while Danny kept saying,

"I would kill you, Pepper! I have a black belt. In karate!"

/* How Katya and I ended up trainspotting in Dubuque, Iowa, on that midsummer Beamer night. */

I spent the afternoon grooming, starting with a much needed wash, then a long nap, followed by a haircut and shave, and lastly a popping of pimples ripe from malnutrition. In the kitchen at home a message waited for me by the phone, a message of paramount importance that read:

"katya called."

When did she call? I wondered. Sometime over the last few weeks, now blurry in the rear view mirror of my life. I dialed her number immediately. She answered with her sweet and sour lemon-lime voice: "Hello?"

"Katya, it's me Johnny."

"Finally returning my call?"

"I've been so busy, Katya; with this project at work."

"Too busy to bother calling back..."

I started to explain. "Let me explain..."

"Doesn't matter," she said, "I'm just wondering when you might stop sending me these flowers."

"Are you still getting flowers?"

"Every Friday. I'm the most popular person at work. I've been donating them to the hospital every week."

"That's terrific! I will continue to send them. Are you busy tonight?"

"Not exactly."

"What is today?" I asked frantically, "Wednesday?"

Katya laughed, "It's Friday."

"Perfect! Let's just get out of the city. I need to get out of the city. Let's hop a freight train and bring a guitar. We can ride on top of the box-cars playing songs. Wear some old jeans. Hobo jeans. Can you play the guitar?"

Katya paused and popped her gum in her mouth. "Did you have a bad week Johnny?"

"Only in my imagination," I said, "What do you say, Katya - should we train-hop and head for nowhere?"

"I admit, it's tempting. But let's go for a drive, we can graduate to the hobo life some other time."

"Ok, my Katya," I said with rising energy, "then let's go for a ride, with the windows down the whole way. Let's flee down the interstate taking random exits. No map, no mile markers, no directions. Definitely no directions. No regulations or parameters, only speed...even if we get caught at least we'll be free for a moment."

"Are you all right?"

"Now I am," I said, "and I want to frolic with you and play with your hair, let's go, I'll pick you up. Do you have to work on Monday?

"Of course I do! Where are we going?"

"That's the idea. I don't know. Pack nothing."

As I drove through Minneapolis on that Beamer night, running last minute errands, everything in the city reminded me of nothing; no place specific. Ubiquitous lights streamed from lamps and neon signs, from molded plastic gold arches, and the department stores blared out 30% savings, no-money-down, no-interest-for-a-year, one-chance-one-day-only sales. Gas stations posted cigarette bargains and trendy restaurant signs crowded the highway. Cars with designer headlights drove toward me in techno blue-green, off-pink, and faded burgundy. All the lights of a city; a city the same as any other city. A sprawling metropolis. I stopped and bought some cigarettes, hoping to get addicted. I filled a small cooler with ice and Budweiser, hoping to get cirrhosis.

Katya sat on the curb outside of her apartment complex, wearing old jeans and a hat, holding a sweatshirt in her lap. I wanted to be near her so much. I wanted to swallow her whole, like a snake would a mouse.

Katya hopped in the car and I drove away. We drove and listened to a baseball game on the radio, quietly enjoying the ride with light conversation and laughs. At midnight, far south of Minneapolis, we sped past Dubuque, Iowa. I kept telling Katya that she and I could do anything we wanted in the world that night. We could go anywhere, we could see anything. Whatever she wanted for that night, in the infinite permutations of reasonable destiny, she would have it done.

"Take a left on that gravel road," Katya ordered.

"Aye, aye," I saluted her.

"Pull into this field road, she said."

"Drive down by the water," she said.

"Get out of the car," she said.

"Isn't this fun?" I said loudly, "We could get shot at for trespassing!"

Katya rolled her eyes, "Yeah, wouldn't that be something?"

Not a single cloud defaced the sky on that October night. The milky way blazed through the night and the middle of our retinas, with no way to tell upside-down or right-side up. The country night spilled with awe on a moonless prairie that led up to the happily rolling Mississippi river.

Katya said, "I've never seen this many stars."

I said, "Not in the city you don't. There's too much illumination in the city to see the night bare, as it should be seen. Maybe too much enlightenment in the city..." My lip quivered a bit as I talked. "Only in the land of the yokels can you find something like this. Us yokels are not as dumb as you might think, Katya, because we have purity like this."

Katya said, "I never called you a yokel, Johnny."

"But I am," my voice wavered as I began to understand my naivety. I said, "I didn't realize how much I had missed the nights. And the grass, and the chirping crickets hiding inside, and the dew," then a tear rolled off my voice onto my cheeks, but I made sure Katya didn't see it.

"It's beautiful, Johnny. This is the most romantic thing anyone's done for me in so long. Maybe ever." She grabbed my hand in hers.

Then of course, I started crying, squinting my eyes tightly in bottomless sadness while the tears squeezed out the sides, and I thought to myself, 'I'm so glad you like it, sweet Katya, because I don't anyone else in the world anymore who would.'

Katya pointed out the constellations as she spotted them. She learned about their formations in a college class at the

University of Minnesota.

"There's Cassiopeia. And Draco."

And I sputtered, "My little brother and I made up our own when we were kids. There's The Cricket, The Caterpillar..."

She laughed as the tears kept crawling out of my squinted eyes, falling for no reason except to fall.

"Katya, I love you," I said.

She looked down at the ground, then looked up at me. She said, "I think...I might be in love with you, too, Johnny Pepper. Although I can't believe I am saying this already."

We stared at each other. In her eyes another milky way swirled, so glorious that I couldn't tell if the galaxy reflected Katya's eyes or she the galaxy. We stared at each other...and suddenly the sound of ten thousand trumpets blasted the moment into chaos.

"JESUS SPOTS, WHAT IS THAT NOISE?!" I said.

"It must be a train!" Katya laughed.

"How did it sneak up on us?"

Our loving moment abruptly postponed as a train came around a curve and blasted a horn forged by the god Vulcan himself. Until then we had no idea railroad tracks were nearby. The track lay only twenty feet away from us.

"Come with me!" Katya said.

Katya ran closer to the tracks and laid supine with her head about a yard from the rail. I shrugged and followed, lying close to the rail with her. The boxcars passed over our heads, blowing and rumbling with sheer force. The power of the train stretched our skin. The horn continued to blare. Lying there I could see boxcars in the top half of my eyesight, and in the lower portion twinkled the peaceful night sky, creating a visual oxymoron. Had the passing train stirred up a rock or branch, we might have died, but we laid there laughing - laughing at the idea of anything ruining our night. The boxcars barreled overhead:

WhooshWhooshWhooshWhoooshWhoosh

Hundreds of cars passed directly over our smiling heads, as we gazed into the moment that we'd discovered.

Katya and I remained still until the caboose passed, but there was no actual caboose. Cabooses no longer append trains, as they've been de-queued in the name of progress. Neither Katya nor I said anything for five minutes, we just held hands, and looked at the stars, until a second train came, and whooshed over us. For that train, I turned my head to watch Katya, to see her smiling at the marvelous view and the unforgettable feeling of power. My life felt relaxed once again. Katya saved me.

With a blanket from the car, we sniggled into the brown grass, tight against each other. A honking train woke us from time to time, allowing us to re-situate our bodies, to get closer, to become a single dot in the universe.

/* What Katya told me in a motel room south of Memphis. */

The following day, we ended up south of Memphis in a motel. After a few drinks, Katya elaborated on her life view while she stood nude on the room's long heater/air conditioner. As she talked, she tip-toed around, pacing to and fro, swinging her foot around poetically to change direction, acting comical while conveying her ideas to me. Also nude, I laid on the bed staring at her wonderful body, attempting to listen.

"You see my whole centerpiece of living is the governance of emotion," Katya said, "and to do so requires discipline. Self-help books promote failure. That's why they remain best-sellers year after year, because the same people keep buying new ones. My point is that living the self-help message is not practical. Two hundred pages of self-help will not fix problems. Three words will: Resolve, humbleness, and acceptance. Have resolve for your undertakings, the humbleness to fail or succeed, and acceptance of the outcome."

I listened nakedly.

"For example," she said, "how many times have you heard the Robert Frost poem about the *The Road Not Taken*? You know the one, 'Two roads diverged in a yellow wood...'"

I said, "I've heard it many times. I've heard it on the news, on TV, from teachers..."

"Exactly. And have you ever heard anyone disagree with the poem?"

"How could anyone disagree with the poem?" I said, crinkling my forehead, "It speaks so obviously about avoiding the path of least resistance - that following the path of least resistance cannot bring gains of anything great."

Katya swung her foot around to change her direction, "But most people are scared to act on that common truism of following their hearts, and if they do believe they've followed their hearts, they are usually wrong. Everyone knows the right things to do; be honest, be unselfish, do not judge others. Everyone *knows* these things in their mind's eye. When the TV news or the book tells us of the crimes and gross actions of certain people, we as viewers nod knowing full well what's right and wrong. And then as listeners we feel superior to the evildoers, but only because many of us haven't been in a situation that would make us commit crime. Everyone has a breaking point, whether they believe it or not. People just want to be happy and when they can't find it they do strange things. And misguided emotions lead to misguided happiness. To crave fame, or rank, or to kill, or steal, or cheat: all are attempts at happiness, but so are the little offenses, like road-rage, overcharging customers, passing judgment on others."

I said, "Then we are all bound to fail at happiness. Is that what you are saying, Katya?"

Katya jumped down from the air conditioner and stood in front of me in her glorious skin.

"We have to fail. We are meant to be sad at times, but we have to withstand life. To live decently without doing anything incredibly dumb; that's my theory."

Rather than delve into the facets of my theory of Containment, I said, "Can we get drunk and make love now, Katya?"

"Yes we can."

/* A season of love and debugging and mass murder. */

Katya and I didn't return to Minneapolis until Monday morning. Though exhausted from driving all night, I went straight to work and started debugging. I fixed a bug that very morning, feeling brilliant despite no sleep.

Riding the high of the weekend, I dreamed of Katya and sent e-mails to her in every spare moment. We discussed the nature of our relationship, and under what parameters dating should proceed. I pored over sonnets and villanelles dedicated to her, so that she might know the great recesses of flattery I had yet to bestow upon her. She modestly accepted my praise and thanked me for such boyish loving. I called her my butterfly; she called me her bee. In the pleasure of the adoring aura, I e-mailed lines to her like: "O, how I wish I could flap my little bee wings out of my office to gather some magic myrrh for you, and fly over to your window and flap until you would see me and let me perch on your tiny finger so I could give you a sweet honey kiss. Then I could fly back to work and never be blue again."

My flowery breeze turned into steel wind when I turned my focus on debugging. By chivalry alone I steamrolled the bugs. I spent a long time in the bowels of the dark code's Containment structure, prodding and poking around, until I managed to stamp my flashing cursor on a guilty process identification number, and then watched it writhe in agony, struggling to increment a guilty variable one last time. I synchronized threads into submission and e-mailed solutions to customers. Another bug slain meant another chance to e-mail Katya regarding my swell of emotion.

For several months, the Beamer nights consisted of only love and debugging, with the evenings being open for Katya and I to take long walks where we held hands and talked for hours.

We went on several vacations, on the spur of a moment. Since I had been working so much and spending no money whatsoever, my savings account accumulated a large quantity of cash for disposal. Yet, the money I spent on trips and gifts for Katya has less value than the moments that cost nothing at all. This fostering of love made these months my favorite Beamer nights due to the plain decency of living. With honesty and pleasure, I can attest to the fact that the memory I own of watching Katya in the city park sitting on a swing opposite of me, with her dark hair playing in the wind of her pendulum motion, and the sound of her laugh permeating the scene, has given me reason to smile during some of the loneliest and darkest of times. Likewise, the times we spent in movie theatres when I secretly watched her instead of the movie, when I watched the light of the amorphous colors of the big screen dance and blend with the natural color of her face, and how I felt her emotions toward the movie reflected in how tightly she squeezed or caressed my hand - these experiences with her I would not trade for all the possessions on earth. From my limited experience, to be in love was the best of all possible worlds.

Love affected my opinion of work as well. Danny went right on reading the news out loud to me, even though he knew I was not listening. His condescension remained intact as well. But this infectious nature of love made me see nothing but joy in every pursuit. Such an emotion, so pure, is love, that it can erase negativity completely from the window of life, to the point that goodness in humanity is all that can be seen by the smitten man. Katya's extension of love made me realize that I am the same as any other man or woman in my needs of love. Mankind inherently harbors good, not evil. How else could this feeling so light and so heavy come to me, if the same ability did not exist in all human beings of the earth?

It was during this period of positive reflection that a group of humans hijacked several airline jets and crashed them into the towers of New York City, burning people alive who were on their way to work, causing a fire hot enough to collapse the entire buildings (with yet more people crushed inside), killing a total of several thousand, wounding thousands more, and subsequently providing the catalyst for a series of wars that had no real objective or enemy but plenty of corpses, and brought much of the world into an apocalyptic frenzy.

Of course, my rosy ideology of humanity stood in shambles after this event, but to my relief, the Beamer corporation quickly took action by sending out an e-mail to all employees, telling us what to do:

"Please do not check the internet for updates on the events that have happened on this traumatic day. The servers are seeing massive performance hits because of employees reading the news. Your manager will keep you updated on what is happening in New York. Try to stay focused on your jobs and the task at hand. The best thing you can do for America is to keep working hard right now."

/* A season of disdain, HTML Cowboying, and vagrancy. */

Katya and I were sad for many days after the destruction and death, with thoughts of love becoming secondary to sorrow. The same feeling of helplessness that dominated so many other Americans ensconced us as well.

The following day after the mayhem in New York, to restore hope and remind us of the Beamer vision, everyone at Beamer attended a diversity meeting. First the emcee of the massive meeting introduced the audience to the panelists who were all seated in front. Each panelist introduced themselves and made a short presentation regarding their section of the diversity pie. I knew that the meeting was especially important for me to attend in order to overcome my proclivity to oppress.

The emcee spent all of the time talking, covering many of the same policies I had learned in Beamer orientation. At the end of the meeting she made a speech about America and the war.

"Now I want to touch on the events that recently happened which shocked all of you, as it did me." She paused and licked her lips. "We are all Americans, or at least work in America, so we all have that in common. In the upcoming weeks we are going to see retaliation by America, in whatever form or forms it is done, and people will probably die in another country. In fact, we can be certain that some form of retaliation will be happening soon. As employees, Beamer needs you to realize that no matter what happens with the war while you are at work, please keep your emotion to yourself. That means, please do not cheer or get angry when you hear about bombings, or acts of terror, or anything related to the war. We have to keep in mind that we are a global company, now more than ever, and you don't want to offend someone who might be from that country, or might have relatives living in that country, or just plain know someone from that country. It's imperative that we respect each other in this time of crisis and focus on the business at hand. If you feel the need to have emotions, please be discrete and go outside."

She smiled and tilted her head at the audience. Everyone attending stayed silent. Most of the Beamers listened and nodded. I listened and nodded.

She said, "We want to be able to do business in the future with the nations we may be at war with. Any questions?"

She smiled and tilted her head the other way. I smiled at her from my seat. The meeting ended. The Beamers filed out in a daze.

In the hallway I heard a voice say, "The worst part about this war will be if the stock price goes down." I turned to look at who could say something so callous, and when I turned, I realized it was Danny that had said it. The horrible words came out of his festering orifice. But several other Beamers standing near him agreed, and started comparing losses in their portfolios since the attack, engaging in a grotesque conversation regarding their hardships.

Which brought me to thinking about the meeting altogether, and how Beamer wanted us to be emotionless. My head spun in confusion as to what was right or wrong. Perhaps this was the beginning of the end.

Back in the office, back to debugging, I stared at the computer monitor at some random code:

```
cntXfer++;
/**********************************************
*****/
/* If bound item is found,  */
/* get current location in  */
/* the container and return it.  */
/* Destroy the head.        */
/**********************************************
*****/
if(plantManifest(itemXt)){
  plink = Container.foo().bar();
  Container.spin().Adhesive.bend();
  ++Container.currentState().rip;
}
else{
  plink = NULL;
}
destabilize(plink, cntXfer, addrConfig,
fnoteScriptStyle)
```

The monitor stared back at me, with its thousands of similar lines queued up for debugging and demoralizing. I knew how to debug, but cared not a jot anymore. The death of so many people sunk my mood. I couldn't even gather the strength to page down. Nothing excited me. Not the bug, not the code, not eating, not sleeping. Not the Shittoon. Not even skydiving. In fact, if at that moment a pyramid of burning dogs water-skied through my office, I wouldn't have bothered to take a second look.

My thoughts shifted from humanism to escapism. And my era of HTML Cowboying commenced.

I continued to work, but at a relaxed pace. Fix a line of code here, save a file there, start a compile, then open the web browser, and flip consciousness...into a land of HTML Cowboying. To where the HTML Cowboy rides the open range of discovery on the internet. To wide open electronic spaces of policy violation.

The HTML Cowboy learns about things. He learns about oil rig jobs. He learns that a roustabout is the lowest form of life on an oil rig. A newbie, in a sense. A roustabout makes coffee and cleans the Shittoons. A roustabout paints walls, greases equipment, wrangles garbage, and cleans up after seamen and floorhands and technicians and engineers. A roustabout must be able to swim, must be in good physical shape, must have a high school diploma, and must have the correct number of chromosomes in every single cell of his body. The roustabout works seven days straight for eleven hours a day, then receives seven days off to defile himself anyway he pleases.

Then the HTML Cowboy thinks to himself: "I could do that job. I could roustabout. I could quit Beamer and head to the Gulf of Mexico or Alaska. I could hang around the docks and beg the foreman for a job plunging toilets. I'd be a roustabout with a college degree. I could do that. I could do that today if I wanted to..."

Then the Cowboy notices that the debugging compile finished running ten minutes ago. He starts transferring the compiled code to another server via FTP.

But the Cowboy tires with waiting for computers to catch up, he loses track of time, and he's already chasing highwaymen in his mind, dreaming of running wild with Willie Nelson or the Outlaws of Trailbaston. He learns the rhymes of an old scallywag trailrunner:

...I shall stay in the woods, in the pleasant shade; there is no false dealing there, nor any bad law, in the wood of Belregard, where flies the Jay,

and the Nightingale sings daily without ceasing...

The HTML Cowboy yearns to be loosed in the woods, living the life of a merry thief, among a people where everyone talks like John Keats, lamenting on anything that moves. Reading the words of the Outlaw he understands; the Outlaw is a hero in the shadows.

You who are indicted, I advise you, come to me, to the green wood of Belregard, where there is no entanglement, just wild animals and pleasant shade; for the common law is too unreliable.

Yes, the common law is too unreliable. To hell with the law. The HTML Cowboy can be a Renaissance rebel if he wants to, living off pawned trinkets and the fruits of stagecoach blitzes.

But back in the Beamer world, my file transfer has finished, and the server's code is updated. The Cowboy must embrace the debug code again, for twenty minutes of problem-solving, but grows disinterested after two minutes...

The law. Yes, the HTML Cowboy could be a dag-gum lawyer if he wanted to. Shit, he can do anything – if he wanted to. The Cowboy could study for the LSAT, and matriculate to law school. But where? The University of Hawaii. On which island? The big island. The city of Hilo has a law school. The Cowboy searches for jobs in Hilo, for apartments in Hilo, and for the cost of transporting his car to Hilo. How will he pay for tuition? He'll pick bananas, or harvest sugarcane, or even be a roustabout swabby on an oil rig and then swim to shore for classes in Hilo. Maybe even learn to surf.

Not internet surfing, real surfing. The Cowboy studies the basics of surfing: how to read tide reports, gearing up, how to spot a sandy beach, how to avoid getting mangled on coral reef, paddling out, duck-diving, the lingo, breathing technique, the dudes, the bush parties, the babes that fall over with their legs in the air...

The debugger hits a breakpoint. The HTML Cowboy typed something wrong. Never mind, he's no longer debugging at Beamer - he's huffing ether straight out of the computer through a narrow straw...

The Cowboy feels a chill. He might be under the weather. Perhaps he has a cold. Perhaps he has cancer. Perhaps he needs to go to the online doctor; a digital diagnostic decision tree. The Cowboy feels tight, like his bowels have been frozen, or like his chest has collapsed. Perhaps an enema would help. But he doesn't know anything about enemas.

So he learns how to self-administer an enema. He learns to hold the quart of water two feet above his stomach so the water can trickle into the colon. (If the Cowboy is a first timer, he'll want supervision with this.) He can lie down during the enema if he prefers. He should hold the water internally for five minutes, and then purge it forcefully. In the enema bag he'll then see large fecal remnants exiting his intestines. Don't fret; this is healthy; this is the whole point of the procedure. He can kneel or stand during this phase of the enema. If at any time the pain becomes unbearable, be sure to monitor the enema release valve. This illustrates why supervision helps. Try to find a companion that regularly flushes himself or herself with an enema. Try not to spill the bag's contents. Feel the cleanliness inside the colon once the procedure finishes? Yes, surely. Perhaps in the future, try more water. Or try lemon juice in the water for a better cleansing effect of the large intestine and anus. Believe it or not, the Cowboy learns, the enema can produce marvelous sexual stimulation, and conversely, excessive gas in the rear can cause unbearable discomfort. Enema bags sell in quantities of one, six, or baker's dozen if the Cowboy wishes to use his Visa or

Mastercard to make a purchase online today.

A compile finishes, and he starts building the program again. The computer stalls in processing.

In the meantime, the Cowboy considers a life in the military. Somewhere with excitement. Anywhere but Beamer! An HTML Cowboy Roustabout Lawyer can do anything in the world. He memorizes the General Orders of the United States Army verbatim.

General order #1: I will guard everything within the limits of my post and quit my post only when properly relieved.

General order #2: I will obey my special orders and...

He reads the Army Ranger handbook. He sees himself as a grunt. He imagines himself in boot camp, regurgitating the General Orders back to the drill sergeant. Yes, he can be anything in the world. He can have a safari in a box. He can play poker with hustlers online. He can flame the government on www.congress.com. He can be a film-yuppie. He can be a beer-snob. He can be a Green-Neoconservative-Libertarian-Mansonist if he wants to, all in the same day.

* * * * *

From that day on, the instant messenger chats permeated every minute of the day. The web browser staggered through web pages by the thousands. I was officially a Beamer policy scofflaw.

Each day of HTML Cowboying ended with my eyes getting heavy, and my thoughts yearning to go home to call Katya. With my tired body, I realized that I really couldn't be a roustabout, that the work on the oil rig would be too difficult for my sagging muscles. As the HTML pipe dreams drifted off into the sunset each day, the comfort of Beamer drew me back to her breast, and I suckled at the teat of the paycheck. To quit Beamer and shed this ease of life? That would be insane. Maybe, instead,

I can have my excitement in moderation, I thought. Yes, I can lasso the vacuum cleaner at home pretending that it's a wild steer. I can plug the toilet at home, then plunge it violently like an oil well. I can watch Perry Mason reruns and know the endings. I can do knuckle pushups during war movies...

Or: I can accept the truth of my Beamer life. I can be a net junky until my ass turns bedsore blue, with the rest of the techies, with the gen-x leftovers, with the newbies, the crackers, the hackers, the gamers, the forum-posters, the fantasy fans, the stock brokers, the cyberpukes, the *Clevertons*, and all the other people searching for something in the void on the world wide web.

Something to fill the waking spaces.

* * * * *

Katya called me to go to dinner one night, to which I answered according to my prevailing mood of that period of time. I said, "Sure. Whatever."

She said, "Well, do you want to do something else? You don't sound too enthused with the idea. We can do anything in the world today, Johnny. Anything at all. Doesn't that excite you? We can drive to Door County or Duluth and stay for a night. We could go watch the Twins lose at the Metrodome. We could go feed the ducks in Minnehaha Park..."

"Or we can just lie here," I interjected glumly.

"Bad day at work, Johnny?"

"I don't know. I don't even know what day it is. Doesn't matter anyway."

"Ok, I feel like I'm talking to a stranger here," said Katya with sarcasm. "I'm going to hang up now. If you want to call me back, go ahead. You're going to have to get out of this funk sooner or later."

"Mmm hmmm." I hung up the phone and didn't call her back.

* * * * *

I recall zoning out in those Beamer nights, working late either at home or the office, staring blankly at my computer monitor until an instant message conversation would pop up. An old college roommate contacted me and we had short conversations almost every evening about our lackluster careers. He too programmed computers but took Prozac and ephedrine to assist his motivation. The work at his company had become as dull as my own. The conversation breathed our *Cleverton* ennui:

roomie: blah.
johnny: blah.
roomie: blah is not word enough. i can't believe i'm at work yet.
johnny: go home then. who's stopping you?
roomie: this job fits like a bad hairpiece.
johnny: can you shave it?
roomie: i can't concentrate on anything with this war going on. all i can think of is useless things. like, today. i kept imagining what life would have been like if J.J. from *Good Times* had guest starred as a boyfriend to the blind girl on *Little House on the Prairie*.
johnny: lol. that's clever.
roomie: i gotta get out of here. there's this greenskeeper job opening up at a local golf course. i've been considering putting in my application.
johnny: do it. or there's always the marine corps if you want excitement.
roomie: julius caesar himself couldn't light a fire under my ass. for dinner tonight I'm having cyanide. organic of course.
johnny: i'd talk you out of it if i didn't agree. i'm plotting my own demise and i will be in the morgue by the time

you get home, due to an intentional collision of some kind.
roomie: lol. see you in hell.
johnny: what do you call this?

* * * * *

Frankly, my attitude sucked.

The only burst of motivation I mustered in that stretch of time was to look out the window at the local vagrant who pushed a shopping cart and sifted through the trash receptacle in front of my house. One night I decided to open the door and ask if I could join him, to which he responded negatively. I informed him that I had no intention of mocking him, but instead I wished to befriend him. He responded gruffly, reminding me that I had the liberty to do whatever I wanted, and let me know that his business was not babysitting. Thus I walked outside and joined the vagrant in his activity of sifting through my trash. The gloves on his hands had so many holes that they'd been reduced to rags, and his shoes stayed together only by the virtue of duct tape. The vagrant pulled out a sack of Mountain Dew cans from my recycling container.

I said, "Do you want more of those cans? I have more empty cans inside."

"I'll take 'em, yeah."

I ran inside and brought out the empty cans, a new pair of gloves, and a pair of Jamie's shoes that looked to be the correct size for the vagrant's feet.

"Do you want these gloves and shoes?" I asked.

"Well...mmm...whaddya gonna charge me for 'em?"

I dangled the gloves and the shoes in my hands, and said jokingly, "I'm gonna charge you an arm...and a leg!"

"If you feel like bein' a smartass, then I don't want 'em."

The joke didn't impress the vagrant. I spent the next few minutes convincing him that no payment was due for the items.

For the rest of the night I followed the vagrant until he finished his collection route, helping where I could in spotting aluminum cans. In some receptacles, mobs of bees hovered on the edges hoping to get inside a Mountain Dew can or other sugar beverage container. On several occasions, a bee had already crawled inside a can that I picked up with my bare hand. High on sugar, the bee would then violently buzz inside the can and startle me due to my bee allergy. The drunken bee would then stumble outside of the can only to hover unsteadily in the air, to wait for the can to be still once again so he could continue the binge. These bees at the garbage cans, I imagined, were supposed to be out searching for flowers and honeysuckle, but had found this refuge of intoxication instead, which voided their work plans for the day. I wondered what the queen bee thought of the workers coming home smelling of Mountain Dew and Yoo-hoo chocolate milk. Surely the bees tried to play it off to the queen, telling her it was just wild honeysuckle or poppy residue, but after a few weeks coming home laden in sugar, well, I'm sure the queen caught on to the worker bees happy-hour tomfoolery. Perhaps the cause of the bees suckling on processed sugar wasn't entirely their fault. The neighborhood lawns around my house had no natural flowers or dandelions or snapdragons (kudos to ChemLawn), leaving the bees little choice but to escape their problems by getting soused in Mountain Dew and Yoo-hoo. Welcome to the real world, bees.

With my help, the vagrant finished going through the neighborhood trash in short time. A few homeowners yelled at us, asking us to leave their trash alone, so I followed the vagrant's lead and walked on to the next trash can. After we scoured enough trash and recycling containers, the vagrant settled down on a bench near a moderately busy street. He put out a sign that read,

> *"Wounded veteran. Can you spare a dime?"*

All the while the vagrant went on ignoring me. Then suddenly he started talking out loud, giving me no clear indication if the words were intended for use in dialogue or monologue. He said, "Jeebus Jeebus Jeebus. You know my father calls me Jeebus no mo...He neveh does. He doesn't. He's a no good sunuffabitch, but he neveh says it. I shoulda listened...I shoulda...neveh 'llowed mysef to get f'sook. Da second time, yes, is wurse den da first. Can't find one man to foller let alone twelf. Nobody even notice."

The vagrant's speech trailed off. I asked as nice as I possibly could, tilting my head to the side and smiling, "What about me? I'm following you. And what all this about your father?"

He looked at me with a confused expression, and went into a different tangent of the story.

"Look at all these sickos," he said. "These selfish...pigs. If I was in charge of this-a hya wold, there wouldn't be'en none of this hya crap."

"Amen to that," I said.

"None of this'n...selfish crap."

"No doubt," I said.

"No prope'ty. Or yawds. Or banks to be puttin' no secrets in. We'd share everathin'."

"What a great world it would be," I said. "Shall we revolt?"

"No favorites or forch-nate sons. We shud be 'llowed to sit here like gent-a-men. And share all that what we has, is, and was. No borders...or bullcrap."

"Then it begins!"

Motorists stopped by and dropped off quarters and dollars for the vagrant. He started to make his bed on the bench by covering himself in newspaper.

I told the vagrant that I just didn't care anymore about debugging at Beamer, and that maybe I wouldn't go to work anymore, but rather I would sift through the trash, collect cans, and smell terrible just like him.

His lips curled apart in contortion as he said, "Lissun to you moanin' bout yer problems. You preachin' to th' choir, boy? Cuz I ain't lissunen to no Beamer cryin on the feet o'me. Hallelujah, Jee-bus, this'n here world jus' turned upside down. Neveh dreamt of the day a rich boy would be pitchin' his complaints at me like I's some kinda fountain. You is plain nuts, I 'magine."

Feeling offended, I said, "But you've probably never had to debug before, sir, and I can assure you that sitting on this park bench watching traffic appeals to me more than watching a computer screen do nothing. I like hanging out here, and I admire your courage to live outside the norms of society."

He yelled back, "What or who in a hell you talkin' about? I's the one tha's livin' out here, not jus' hangin' out. Get on back to yo fuggin' de-buggy house! Dis here neighb'hood right here, is 'bout 'nuff to make me sick, den you come 'round long 'nuff to make it wursen."

Not believing his anger to be authentic, I pressed on, hoping to learn more about the man. "Do you mind if I ask what war you served in?"

His head jerked up. "War? What ta hell you talkin' 'bout, boy?"

I pointed to his sign.

"Well, it were the War o' 1812. Get yo ass outta hya!"

I laughed at his joke. "You must be almost two hundred years old by!"

"Older. You's a mutha of a prick, ain't ya, boy?"

"I don't mean to be a prick," I laughed, "Or any other kind of phallis. I'm sure we'll get along fine in time. Would you mind if I hang out with you tomorrow? I'll bring some sandwiches and potato chips. Maybe a deck of cards."

He spat on my shoe, and said, "What do I look like? The fuggin' govuh-ment to you? You can do wheteveh ta hell pleases ya. I ain't gonna force no man to do nuth-in'! I'm done with all that. Git on outta here nah!"

Out of my respect for the man, I went home in accordance to his wish.

The next day I decided to skip work at Beamer in order to attend the park bench, where I put out my own sign and collection hat so that I might receive a taste of the donations from the passing motorists. I printed the 'Wounded Veteran' sign out at home, with large letters in Impact font type.

Several motorists stopped and offered a few coins or a dollar to my fund. From underneath my newspaper bed on the bench, I voiced my thanks to each contributor and inquired whether he or she needed any change, but each declined or simply gave me a strange look. Later, in the afternoon, when the vagrant arrived, I jumped to my feet, bursting forth from beneath the newspapers to tell him that I had already earned seven dollars and twenty-seven cents over the course of the day. Earning that seven dollars felt much better to me than the four hundred dollars Beamer was paying me during those same hours.

Quite opposite of the reaction I expected from the vagrant, he bullrushed me and snatched the money-hat right out of my hands.

"Now who'n a hell does you think you is anyways? Dyou jus' think you can come a steal a man's place?"

I pleaded, "But just yesterday you said we should share everything..."

He lunged at me with his words, causing me to flinch like a coward. "Oh, now you wanna get to be a smartass! I'd remembah if I said sumthin' stupid as that. I said nuth-in' of the sort. Nuth-in! This here is my spot! Don't go gettin' no cute ideas, nah. Uh-uh. You jus' take that thievin' ass of yours sumwherz else. This hya my spot."

I argued, "But you said there should be no property..."

At which time he heaved a leaking bag of aluminum cans at my head. I dodged the bulk of the bag, but one of the cans ejected toward me from the airborne bag, and from the can, a bee that had been suckling on the pop-top detached his little body and landed on my face. I screamed, but the wee drunkard pointed his venomous stinger right into my lower lip. I scampered off toward my house to get my syringe and needle antidote, hoping to inject myself with epinephrine before my throat and mouth swelled shut. Afraid of dying and confused as ever, I suddenly realized that I had yet to learn anything concrete about the thought processes of mankind. Yet my philosophy was choked--thank goodness--by the onset of anaphylaxis, and I writhed in a neighbor's yard, gaping for air like a hungry baby bird.

/* A season of loss, a season of madness. */

My attitude worsened further. The blandness increased in my interactions with Katya, who often inquired into the cause of my weary demeanor, but I spurned her entreaties with jaded answers. I recall seeing her eyes plead for a return to normalcy. Her eyes said, "Where is the Johnny Pepper that kissed me at the Christian party, and laid with me by the trains?" But no suitable answer came to my lips, for my heart felt like a cold stone in a winter field. The world had nothing to offer but flat plains when I'd come to expect mountains and rapids. It was too late for me, being so naive as to take myself seriously.

The fact that Katya bothered to stay with me during those Beamer nights is testimony of her dedication to our relationship. However hard she tried, whether in suggesting activities to do or in trying to arouse me bodily, I tried just as hard to avoid movement of any kind.

The Beamer's surrounding me fared poorly, too. Fillmore received her layoff notice. Beamer gave her a week to gather her things and leave the premises. It was the sixth round of layoffs in my two years at Beamer. The manager sent a continuous barrage of e-mails to the department heralding the company's prosperity, yet Beamer laid off employees every few months. On one hand, I wondered why Fillmore's day hadn't come sooner and on the other hand I felt sorry for the herbivore. During the time I'd worked at Beamer, she had pawned many bugs to me as she evaded work, but still, somehow the whole process seemed to lack any consideration, and continued to bludgeon at whatever little employee dedication remained.

Danny tilted his head at Fillmore in falsetto sympathy. "I'm sorry to hear about this, Fillmore. What are you going to do now?"

"I don't know," Fillmore sighed. "My husband still has a job, so we should be able to get by during the interim while I send out applications. Or Beamer might hire me back in a month. That's the latest rumor."

"Hire you back? Then why let you go at all?" I asked.

Fillmore bobbed her long face, "Well, apparently sometimes they lay people off and hire them back."

Danny said, "Yes, of course. To cut costs for a temporary time."

I grew agitated, "So you are just supposed to put life on hold?"

Fillmore looked down, "I guess."

I exclaimed, "How can Beamer expect any motivation or work to be done by anyone, when they do random layoffs for no good reason but to look good on paper?"

Danny said, "The finance department has a fiduciary responsibility to the stockholders."

Danny and Fillmore tilted their heads at me.

Then I said something immediately regrettable due to the derogatory nature. I said, "Then God damn finance should make more conservative estimates of future revenue. I mean, Fillmore never missed a day, even if she is a lazy, obese horse. And why hire her back at all if she's just going to do the same job, sitting here talking to you all day, Danny? I can't find any inspiration here when a greasy, lifeless paycheck is the only motivator. That and our merit less annual bonus." Yes, I was too high strung, a dandy of sorts, an idealist.

For once Danny and Fillmore were both silent. Fillmore looked sad after my horse comment, but the silence assured me that both her and Danny were more paycheck driven than I. I suppose work of any kind at some point is just a paycheck, whether you work in a morgue or a circus.

At noon I left the office for the day. On the drive home I thumbed through my wallet looking for a video rental card, thinking that renting several movies and doing nothing would be a good way to spend an evening. I came across the phone number for Jeff, one of the drywallers from the night I met Katya. I picked up my cell phone and called him.

"Yallow," Jeff answered.

"Jeff...this is Johnny Pepper. Remember me?"

"Who?"

"I'm the guy who watched you fall down the staircase. Remember me, and Katya?"

A pause followed by a laugh came across the airwaves. "Oh, I do somewhat remember you. That was a rough night."

I asked, "How's your head?"

"Fine now. It hurt for about a week. It took lots of pain killers and blunts to get me through."

Then I asked the question that led me to the demise of reason: "What are you doing tonight? You want to go pound some beer?"

He said, "I was just thinking the same thing. This house I'm working on is finished. Why wait until tonight? Let's go right now."

He mentioned a bar that I could meet him at, so I steered my car in his direction.

We sent ourselves overboard, off the plank into an ocean of booze, until late into the afternoon and early evening. The construction workers and their girlfriends poured into the bar. I felt content seeing no Beamer tilted heads or lilted voices. The cigarette smoke plumed into a blue cloud in the center of the barroom. The men playing pool sank nearly every shot they attempted, even the shots involving difficult angles. The dart board lit up with bulls-eyes. And a man sitting next to me held a spit cup for his snuff tobacco in one hand while he held a beer with his other hand. I asked his name, and he said his friends called him 'Killer.' (Or maybe it was 'Knife,' I can't recall.) One of Killer Knife's friends asked if I rolled dice, to which I said, "I used to roll dice in college."

"Hey, look at this guy, Killer Knife, we got a college boy here."

"Oh yeah?" Killer Knife said, "Well his money's good, too. Ok, college boy, let's roll some dice. Five bucks a round."

I asked the bartender to break a one hundred dollar bill for me, which evoked whistles from Killer Knife and his friend.

After my turn at rolling dice, I quietly asked Killer Knife's friend how a nickname like Killer Knife's came to him.

Killer Knife's friend answered, "Cuz he killed a couple dudes a few years ago...allegedly." Then he winked at me twice and said, "Why, are you a cop or something?"

"No, I'm a Beamer."

"Good. Then you're not much of a threat, right? Ha ha! No, I'm just jokin' with ya."

Later, a fight broke out near my barstool. I watched and smiled, enjoying the fact that places still existed in America where people had fistfights. I continued smiling until the fight broke up, then one of the fighters said to me, "What are you lookin' at...do you want to be next, huh, freak?"

I turned away from the steel-blue gaze of the fighter, but I continued smiling, now with my own fist clenched, clenching not out of anger but out of joy. I thought to myself - 'I would like to be in a fight with one of these gentlemen.' And I proceeded to consume so many drinks that the opportunity lent itself to me as if by design. The opportunity came when Shawna, the adulterer I adulterated showed up at the bar. With her husband.

She strolled up to the end of the L-shaped bar and sat down so that we could see each other. The husband stood close behind her stool. The size of the husband did not intimidate me as it would have earlier in the day, because through drink I had grown stronger, taller, and better looking. Funnier even. I tapped Jeff the drywaller to tell him about what had happened with the lusty Shawna and I on that lonely Beamer night.

Jeff warned, "Stay away from the married ones, Johnny. Believe me, I know. It's a bad idea, always. There is *never* a good outcome from such a thing. Well, that's not entirely true. There is never a good outcome except for my ex-wife and her new husband. I guess it worked out pretty well for them." He laughed.

The hiccups interrupted my eloquence. I said, "But her husband is the guy that <hic> treats her like crap all the time. That's what she told me."

Jeff sneered. "Oh, shee-it, Johnny! They all say that stuff. Ask any woman while she's having problems with her man, and they'll all say they are getting the worse end of the stick. But that don't mean it's the truth. Men say the same lines, just in different ways. Everybody's got selective perception, man. She wouldn't have cheated on him if all was well, now would she?"

Not heeding Jeff, I told the bartender to put Shawna's drinks on my tab. When the husband learned that his drink came from me, he responded favorably by holding up the Schmidt's bottle in appreciation. In response, I extended my hand and lifted my middle finger at him, expecting this gesture to produce the bellicose environment I desired, so that I might beat up the husband or be beaten up by him. The husband looked confused, then amused. He affably attempted to play off my aggression as a joke. Shawna then noticed me, and her face turned beet-red. She smiled painfully at me and offered a little wave of her hand, but then looked away from both me and the husband. The husband caught a glimpse of Shawna's little wave and I read his lips whispering to her, "How do you know that guy?"

Shawna's voice was drowned in the clinking of glasses, the clattering of pool balls, and the music of the jukebox. By the gesticulations of Shawna and the vigorous finger pointing of the husband, I knew they were arguing with subdued voices. The husband put his mouth next to Shawna's ear and he jawed away in interrogation, causing her to sit with a bitterly ill expression on her face, until she reached up with her hand and shoved the husband's head out of her personal space. Undaunted, the husband replaced his head by her ear, only for her to paw him off again. Then the husband walked to where I sat, giving me a fit of nervousness to go with my foolhardy idiot grin. He stood right behind my barstool, and said, "How do you know my wife?"

I ignored him.

He said, "Hey numb-nuts! I'm talking to you."

Jeff turned around on his barstool and said, "Whoa! There's no need to talk like that. Relax, man."

"I'll relax when he answers me," said the husband. "How do you know my wife?"

I turned on my barstool and said, "Are you addressing me?"

"Answer the question. How do you know my wife?"

I took a drink, then set my drink on the bar, and said out loud, "How do I know your wife? Is that what you're asking?"

"Yes."

"I know her by her bare ass."

Then the husband's giant fist bent my nose flat. In the flash, his knuckles became bright red. I threw my fist at his mouth as he hit me, and my bundle of knuckles pushed his upper lip under his upper teeth so that one of his teeth punctured right through his upper lip! When I recoiled, I saw blood rivulets seeping down his incisors, which boosted my fighting confidence. I had wounded him, but the husband hit me again, and cleanly busted my nose. The crowd loved it. Blood poured onto my white plaid Beamer shirt. Killer Knife and Jeff jumped forward and ended the fight for the moment.

Jeff said, "Johnny, you're a moron. Do you know that? Remember that guy we stopped from wasting you in the dance club? Now you are acting just like him! Like an ass!"

The husband said, "You. Outside. Let's go outside. I'm not done with you."

I yelled, "No, I'm not done with you, fartknocker!!"

Shawna pleaded, "Johnny, don't go outside." She stood in front of me, blocking my path. Her voice shook her breasts. "Johnny, do not go outside. He'll hurt you." I pushed past Shawna. The moment was epic; she was Andromache and I was Hector. I went out to meet Achilles.

I stepped into the cold air like a great warrior, ready to slay or be slain. The flaccidity of my muscles rippled like veal and my nipples stood on end. Snow had started to swirl. I wore my blood as a red badge of courage on my shirt pocket and sleeve. Like a lion in the pit I prepared to gouge and shred the gladiator, and the fear in his eyes made itself known to me. He would know the name Johnny Pepper before I performed my finishing move. The bar patrons gathered in the standard semi-circle to watch the great duel between the warriors. They wanted to watch a Beamer try to fight, and the crowd got precisely the showing to be expected.

It was a debacle. I crumpled under the very first blow

from the husband and bled like a stuck hog (as my father used to say). Alas, the gods had lured me to my destruction! He had the decency to punch me several more times in the face before I had a chance to beg his forgiveness. In the end I lay supine on the gravel parking lot staring up and waiting for the beasts of battle to begin gnawing and tearing at my flesh.

Shawna said to her husband, "Are you happy now, Jason? You're hand is probably broken and you won't be able to work. You just...God...you just...couldn't let it go, could you?"

The husband, who I learned was named Jason, said, "And you couldn't keep your legs together, could you, Shawna?"

The crowd snickered and hooted as they shuffled back inside the bar. I rolled onto my stomach in order to secretly cry and watch my blood speckle the ground like a Jackson Pollack artwork, which might have been aptly titled: "Pile of Myself."

Jason said, "Shawna - I don't even care what you do today, tomorrow, or forever from now." He pushed open the bar boor and faded into the blue cloud of smoke.

Jeff said to me with a laugh, "Boy, you asked for that beating. Dare I say it, Johnny, but he got his justice."

"Leave me alone," I muttered.

Jeff laughed on as he pulled me to my feet. He asked, "Are you all right now, dude? Your face is a damn mess. Honestly, I've never seen anyone get hit so square in the face. And the best part was that you didn't even attempt to avoid it!"

Shawna remained outside in the cold. Standing at my side, she said to me, "I'm sorry Johnny. I never told him about us. You shouldn't have said anything and he never would have found out."

"Oh good, Shawna," I cried, "then we could are liars as well as cheats."

"Oh, Johnny. I'm so sorry. But now you see what a horrible person he is."

"Just like you and me!" I blubbered in anguish.

She picked me up and walked me to my car with her arm draped over my shoulder. She wiped my face clean and asked if she could drive me home. I shrugged and got in the car. On the drive to my house Shawna sobbed, lamenting on her broken life, commenting on what is and what never will be, scorning the fact that she settled down too early in life and had nothing to look forward to.

When she reached my house she became my nurse, put ice on my head, told me to lie down. She kissed me on the forehead.

* * * * *

Katya, from here I hardly need go on with this rendition of Beamer nights because you already know this event too well, and probably never wish to hear it in detail again. But I plan on including it here for the sake of honesty, so that I can convey the truth of my inner thoughts to you, and leave nothing untold.

* * * * *

Throughout the night, Shawna watched over me in my bedroom, partially concerned for me and partially to avoid going across the street to her husband. She started trying to kiss my neck, and I said no, but she went on kissing, and before long I enjoyed the attention. However, after a minute of this hopeless pleasure, I thought of you, Katya, and slowly pushed Shawna away from me. At that point I rose from the chair, went to my room, put on a pair of shorts, laid down in my bed, and fell asleep on contact with the pillow.

I remember that morning, Katya...waking up with that hammering headache and rolling over to a voice coming from a figure standing in the doorway of my bedroom. I recognized the voice as yours, Katya, and it filled me with the full feeling of love that I hadn't felt for many Beamer nights, possibly since the war began. It was the yearning that comes to a guilty man who sees the error of his way and hopes to have everything return to normal. I opened my eyes, expecting to see you smiling at me, but instead you said nothing and wore a blank face. You stood holding a plate of pancakes in one hand, and a bottle of Aunt Jemima maple syrup in the other. You stood motionless with your mouth shut.

I said, "Katya, I'm so glad to see you. I had the worst night. My head hurts so bad..."

"Johnny...I can't..."

"What, Katya? What is it?"

"I can't believe...I can't...believe. And here...all this time I just thought you were depressed...but instead you've been. I just can't...I can't believe..."

"What is it? What can't you believe, Katya?"

"You."

Then Katya, you let out a short and defeated laugh, dropped the pancakes and syrup bottle onto the carpet...and then you were gone, Katya. When I sat up in bed to stop the syrup from spilling, I looked to my left, and there lay Shawna, completely nude. My stomach churned in discontent and I threw up bile onto the syrup still flowing onto the floor, and my head exploded internally from pain and shock.

I prodded Shawna awake and asked her to leave my life forever.

/* How I decided to write the virus called Staphlopopeye. */

For the next week, I spent my time trying to call you, Katya, leaving message after message, and I guess you took notice because soon enough my phone number was blocked from calling your phone number altogether. The entire week I stayed at home, in agony of losing you and to avoid having to explain my raccoon eyes to Danny and the manager at work. I wrote those long letters you received in the mail, Katya, pleading for forgiveness, but you only responded once with the terse reply that read:

"Johnny, I can't forgive you, and I think you have too much growing up to do and experiences yet to go through before you will be ready for anything serious. I really did love you, but it's over.

love, Katya"

That same week, Jamie, my roommate, moved out of my house, citing irreconcilable theological differences as the cause for the split. His piety had continued to grow in direct proportion to his overcharging of Beamer customers. I offered no objection to his decision and wished him luck.

I decided that solitude is bliss.

Frequenting the Shittoon became as normal for me as skipping work, and by skipping work, I mean not showing up at all. Occasionally I missed several consecutive days only to return to find a stack of e-mails from other Beamers asking me questions on certain issues, but I never received reprimand or punishment of any kind for my truancy. One day I came into work for an hour just to receive a department award presented to me, for a bug I had fixed months before. After the meeting I walked right back out the door, and went to a double matinee at the nearest movie theater. Over the course of three years, even with all the HTML Cowboying and days spent instant messaging, I had become an expert of sorts, making me wonder just how little the other Beamers in my department really worked. As the sole voice of reprimand, Danny made comments about my sloven appearance and inquired to my whereabouts, but I disregarded him as an entity of any kind, not worthy of an answer. For all the time Danny and I shared the office, never once did I hear a positive comment exit his lisping oral cavity.

Loathing Danny became a dark obsession.

I spent as little time as possible in the office near Danny, but even in the sanity and sanctity of the Shittoon, reminders of Danny festered. I scorned the day of his birth, or hatching, into this world. The things Danny had read out loud off the internet spawned parasites in my head:

"The gas price in Denver is a dollar ninety-nine. What a screw."

"'Ear cloned on mouse.' What's next? Butts? Butt cloned on mouse. I can see it now."

"'Mad cow disease increases airport spending.' Yep, more of my tax dollars wasted."

"'Heavy protesting in Canada.' Christ, America should just make it the 51st state."

Shivers riddled my spine as the fragmented headlines raked the inner walls of my cranium. How did Danny get here? Without being fired? Without the public lynching him? I was convinced that he was born from his mother's anus. And that his fetus started as only an anus and as a deformity his body grew from a sprig of shit.

Hate. Reckless hate. The unnamable. The uncontainable. It boiled inside me like volcanic magma, until I spewed my derisions, and I damned all the things of the world that aided Danny's continuation of breathing. I damned the wretched soil that grew the food that would feed his mealy mouth and oxygenate his cells. I held my breath to avoid breathing the air of the earth he had already befouled. I yearned for a blight on the cotton fields that grew the fabric for his t-shirts, and for mad-cow disease to strike death and rot upon the leather destined for his shoes; for the oil pumps to malfunction and explode that brought crude oil to the surface on its way to Danny's automobile; for the artesian well to dry up that belched his pompous designer water; for the writer of a story that could be adapted into a movie that Danny might someday enjoy, yes, for that writer to develop lumbago, rheumatoid arthritis and carpal tunnel syndrome so that his crooked self could not create the words; for the Beamer servers to crash so that Danny could no longer read news items out loud.

For the servers to crash…now that was an idea.

* * * * *

I needed a name the public might remember for a few years. A name like Codeskunk. Bacillibomb. Monitor Jaundice. Scrabs. Staphlopopeye.

The spore actually emanated from a comment Danny made.

He had claimed, "Think of how easy it would be to plant a virus in this source code somewhere. I could write one in ten minutes."

True, even Danny could write code to crash a server, because anyone can write faulty code. But crashing the server in style and hiding the evidence makes the process difficult. It requires a great plan. And to have a virus forever attached to your name, then you might as well do something worthwhile. I considered running a denial-of-service attack from inside the WebCutter code, but the technique seemed old hat. I found something better, different, more complex, and more lethal.

Memoirs of a Virus Programmer

First off, I needed Danny's password, which proved to be almost as difficult as writing the virus itself, due to the anxiety it caused me. I had to create a temporary website that looked exactly like the Beamer intranet homepage, which changed its appearance on a daily basis. Danny's browser was always set to open the Beamer website, and he previously admitted to me in one of his ramblings that he used only one password for his access at Beamer. The same password for everything.

My nerves tightened with joyful excitement, my fingers trembled as I wrote my program after hours. Writing the virus code thrilled me, my eyes stayed glued to my monitor. In my chair, I leaned so far forward to the computer screen, that I had to put a knee on the carpet. On several occasions, I leaned out my chair far enough, that I fell clear out of the chair onto the office floor in a heap. My fingers danced and plucked at the keyboard like a harpist's, and with more creativity than I'd ever had debugging. Programming became downright wonderful because for the first time since the cancellation of the Asian-Irishwoman's project, my inflated Beamer title of 'software engineer' was applicable.

On the day I lifted Danny's password off him, I waited for him to leave the office for a minute without locking his computer. Rarely did he leave his computer without protecting the password, so I had to be patient. As soon as he left it unprotected, I shut the office door and jumped into his chair to install my theft program that I named *Snort*. Simply sitting in Danny's chair made me feel putrid, thinking of the cemetery of flatulence he'd buried in the pad of his chair over the years. It revolted me and therefore I worked quickly, with efficiency. From a floppy disk I copied my program to his hard drive, then ejected the disk immediately and tossed it onto my desk. My biggest fear was leaving my disk in his floppy drive for him to discover upon return. With the physical evidence safely on my desk, I followed my checklist.

Do list:
a.) Create environment variables and set PATH to include my evil.
b.) Change homepage on the browser to my *Snort* loader.
c.) Test the socket. Run the code in his browser.
d.) Copy cleanup script that will clean the environment and reset browser homepage.

To test the code I had to spin my chair back and forth between my computer and Danny's. Suddenly the door handle started to turn; Danny had returned from his walk early! I scrambled to push my empty chair into the door to block his entrance.

From outside the door, he said, "Excuse me? This is my office more than yours. I shouldn't have to wait to get in my own office."

While he nagged, I held my chair stiff against the door with one hand and with the other hand I changed his computer monitor back to the original look. Quietly I rose from Danny's chair, and moved my body back into my own chair by the door.

Danny entered and sat down none the wiser. He started complaining in classic form, compulsively and with no purpose.

"The Beamer CEO should be fired by the board of directors," he said, "If he'd take a look at the stock price once in a while, maybe he'd get something done. Right now my stock options are in the toilet. If I exercised them right now, I'd lose 3,000 dollars."

"Shut up you filthy animal," I thought to myself.

Since Fillmore fell under Beamer's layoff ax, Danny expected me to become his sounding board for his nagging on socioeconomic issues, but I never gave him the satisfaction of a single rebuttal or agreement.

My pores exuded anticipation as my first experience of

password theft neared. Danny continued his grating diatribe against the Beamer stock price, but I smiled into my monitor, waiting for the precious password to come to me. He kept on griping.

"We should do away entirely with social security," he opined. "Everyone should plan their own retirement. If they forget to plan it themselves, let them starve when they're old. That's what I think. There's no excuse anymore for not planning your own retirement."

Danny surfed the web, avoiding work, avoiding my Snort program. An hour of waiting for him to hit the right web address festered eternally, but the moment materialized at last. Danny's mouse cursor clicked the 'Home' button on the browser, and through the instantaneous highways and transports built into his machine, Snort loaded into his web browser, activating my program. When he opened Snort, the program sent a notification to a listening socket on my machine so I knew exactly what was going on. I peered over my shoulder to watch the know-it-all Danny get sucker-punched. The password prompt appeared in front of him, looking exactly the same as the Beamer password prompt - I made certain of the details. Over my shoulder I wanted to scream maniacally, to laugh out loud, but somehow I maintained composure.

He typed the password. When he hit the enter key, the password string transferred to my computer instantaneously. I had the secret word, which was:

clairi0n

"Nice password, Danny," I silently mocked. It was a combination of his wife's name and a musical instrument from one of his fantasy or science-fiction games. The cleverness made me loathe him murderously.

To be safe, my program indicated to Danny that he had entered the wrong password, so he was forced to enter it a second time. I received confirmation of the password when he entered the word again:

clairi0n

My program, still running on his machine started to self-cannibalize to erase itself. When my main program thread stopped executing, a small batch program named *Felcher* deleted all of my files on Danny's computer, reset Danny's web browser homepage, reset the environment, and left only the batch file itself, *Felcher*, in an obscure directory path. Nothing in that file could ever make sense to anyone due to the screwy naming scheme I gave to my variables. *Felcher* remained dumb and dormant on Danny's computer.

Moving into phase II of the viral insertion, I spent days in a paranoid programming paradise. Using Danny's password I logged into the servers he normally used. I only made changes to the files during the day when Danny walked the halls or went to lunch because the Beamer software recorded a timestamp and a username for every single change made to the files of WebCutter source code. The times that I made code changes needed to reflect when Danny actually attended work. If I'd changed the files at midnight and Danny hadn't swiped his Beamer badge at the building entrance since the early morning, something would have looked awry. Software detectives can find mundane clues with ease, and I had no intention of making their job easy.

In a directory of code that Danny frequently pretended to work on, I looked for my viral insertion point. I opened and closed many files as I searched for a file perfectly obtuse, a file that no one really understood or cared about any more. (Of course, once my virus crashed the systems, Beamer would certainly care about the code. Someone like Ted would be able to figure out my little party crasher, no matter how obtuse or how many diversions I put in the code to lead him astray from the core of the bug.) After an hour of searching, a file captured my imagination, one with several thousand lines of code to act as camouflage for the thread I dropped in. A thread can do all kinds of wonderful, useful jobs in the programming world. To activate the thread, I needed to have a kickoff point, a hook, somewhere else in the code. The activation needed to be senseless and confusing enough that no programmer coming across it would want to consider wasting his time monkeying with it. I created a hexadecimal variable that equaled the date of January 1st, and to make it look good I inserted the joke of a comment:

/* Y2K Compliance Fix# STPHLPPY */

Anyone looking at the code would have passed right over my code based on the comment alone, since, we as programmers, spent thousands of hours in boredom fixing bugs and prayed to never look at them again. No programmer had the time or the energy for a senseless goose chase into decade-old code.

With my hexadecimal variable set to New Year's Day, I next did a series of bewildering multiplications, divisions, and bitwise operations to arrive at a more suitable date for the virus to activate - which was Danny's birthday...which happened to be one week before the end of the third fiscal quarter, which happened to be the perfect time for a Dow stock to take a dive and rattle Wall Street. On that date, when the function executed, my thread would activate, printing out the words on the WebCutter console in typical Beamer green text:

"YOU HAVE CONTRACTED STAPHLOPOPEYE."

After the printout, a dynamic generation-compile-load of a tiny executable would attempt to call a native function from outside the active WebCutter program, but the function invoked would not exist, and crash the whole system. From the first bug I fixed, from my "pointer to a pointer" bug, I knew this type of error crashed Beamer WebCutter as well as the physical server itself. No one knew about my "pointer to a pointer" fix; not even the customers for whom I had built the original workaround knew the details. Also, when I tried to explain this same error to Danny and Fillmore, they had ignored me. Ted never asked me about my final solution to my first bug, so even he didn't know. No digital or paper trail existed on the topic. The virus created total WebCutter failure, so that the WebCutter application would not restart; yes, I made sure of that by rewriting parts of key WebCutter startup files, adding hooks for my code, so that I could replace useful bytes with garbage binary that spelled the word '*MONKEYWRENCH.*' That ensured an irrecoverable error on the launching of Beamer WebCutter.

Lastly, to confuse the lucky Beamer who would earn the privilege of debugging my virus, I decided to start ten thousand threads of Staphlopopeye before I allowed the machine to actually crash, just so the Beamer debuggers could spend a day or three trying to determine if a memory leak had caused the crash.

After the virus would finish its execution, in the post-crash hours, any business running WebCutter would require professional system administrators to recover their lost data. Also, businesses would need Beamer administrators and consultants to reinstall the entire application - for free. My virus was a one-shot-one-day-only deal, much like a sale at Nordstrom's. But WebCutter applications would stay pinned down for at least a day, and possibly up to a week or more. Every company using Beamer WebCutter would require professional help to re-install their wonderful, reliable Beamer product. All Beamer WebCutter applications would fail at the exact same time – noon, Central Standard Time. Thousands of web sites would be disabled and millions of *Clevertons* would be refused their beloved connections! They would be forced to engage in conversation with other humans via phone or face-to-face. I imagined a national news story, with Danny's sick dimpled-chin peanut-head getting discussed in every home.

To insure chaos, I did a quality assurance test of the code

on one of Danny's servers, then I formatted the entire system to erase my tracks.

A day later, when Danny walked the halls, I copied clues to his hard drive for the FBI to discover when they scanned his system. I planted a text file on his hard drive as well, with the 'brainstorming' Danny had done on Staphlopopeye and other viruses:

Monitor Jaundice - a diseased PC that corrupts the rendering of graphics.

Staphlopopeye - a condition of bulging eyes stemming from lost data.

Scrabs - a itching sensation from finding thousands of empty text files written into the directory trees.

I even spoofed Danny's home e-mail address from his work address (now that I knew his password). I sent spoofs from Danny's computer to disconnect myself entirely from the e-mail. To spoof is to blatantly falsify the address of the e-mail sender so it appears to originate from someone other than the actual sender. Had I sent a spoof from my system and Danny failed to delete the message, someone could still figure out that the e-mail originated from me. Why did I send the spoofs to Danny? To increase the chances that Danny would fail a polygraph test with the FBI. I sent spoofs once a week. Each time Danny read the spoofed message, I expected him to subconsciously remember the word 'Staphlopopeye.' He would certainly discard the message as SPAM, and if he didn't delete the e-mails, investigators would only find Danny had spoofed himself. The message I spoofed Danny with read as follows:

From :   "Staphlopopeye." <staphlopopeye@taphlopopeye.com>

To :   <dannyb@gamernet.com>

Subject :   RE: STAPHLOPOPEYE

****

Not much of a man? You need STAPHLOPOPEYE? If interested call 1-800-STAPHLO-POPEYE.

****

Danny was framed. And I laughed, not so much from thinking of the crash of every Beamer WebCutter in the many thousands of businesses all at once, but I laughed thinking of Danny getting grilled by the FBI, his pompous attitude stomped to nothing, and his total uselessness biting him in the rear at last. I expected the FBI to question me extensively as well, since I was the digital felon's office mate. So I practiced lying every day, hoping that my statements could lead to imprisonment for Danny. While at work, I concentrated on learning to lie and how to beat polygraph tests. I started placing a flat steel tack up through the sole of my shoe so that the tack dug into the sole of my foot. I practiced stepping on the point, like stepping on a car accelerator, until my pressure on the tack initiated the exact same amount of pain each time in order to deceive a polygraph machine. If the FBI made me take off my shoes during a polygraph test, I had prepared for that contingency as well. A smaller flat tack fit nicely into a gap in the rear of my mouth where one of my wisdom teeth had been. When I spoke, the tack speared the gums surrounding my molars, causing a nice wincing pain throughout my entire body. The tack hurt my mouth terribly, but to bring Danny to justice motivated me enough to endure the stigmata of Christ if I had to. Practice makes perfect. Danny needed to be corrected in a correctional facility. A few years behind bars would shut his mouth. And I could only dream that the sodomites in prison would make Danny their love slave and ream his ass daily.

After closing the file for the last time, I smiled at my

reflection in my monitor. Then I asked Danny what the cafeteria was serving for lunch.

"Tater-tot hot dish," Danny sneered. "It probably has rancid meat in it. I can just see those idiot workers down there buying their wares at some liquidation meat sale or something."

I felt the tack in my mouth stab my gums -

"HA HA HA!" I yelled gaudily, "that's a good one, Danny!" I laughed on and on ridiculously.

Danny said, "Jeepers, it wasn't that funny."

I smiled maliciously at my monitor knowing exactly what was funny.

The manager walked past the office and heard me laughing. He peered into the office and asked, "What's so funny in here? Did I miss a good joke?"

Seeing an opportunity to be a nuisance, I said, "You sure did. You'd have to ask Danny tell the joke again. He sure knows how to tell a good joke. Tell him the one you just told me, Danny. Tell the one about the Jew, the Ethiopian, and the fat retard."

"I didn't tell a joke," Danny scoffed, "Johnny's lying."

"Oh, come now, Danny," I pushed, "don't try to sweep it under the rug. I just heard you say it a minute ago."

The manager looked at Danny and said, "I hope this joke was tasteful. Otherwise I'd rather not hear it."

Danny grew agitated and said, "Johnny's lying. I don't know any jokes..."

I butted in, "Fine, Danny, I'll tell him if you want to pretend you didn't say it." I looked at the manager and said, "Danny just finished saying it when you walked by. Heck, I'm still laughing. He said...heh heh...hold on a minute," I slapped my knee for effect. I said, "Ok. So there's this cheap Jew, a black-as-ink Ethiopian, and a Vegetable..."

The manager stopped me immediately from going on with the joke, fortunately for me because I knew of no joke that started off with such a trio of prejudice. The manager said, "Ok, I don't need to hear this joke. Johnny - would you come to my office for a minute. I need to speak to you."

"Certainly," I laughed and slapped Danny on the shoulder. I said, "Getting out of this office will give me a chance to recover from Danny's comedy hour."

The manager flashed Danny a dirty look before we walked out, causing Danny to squirm in his chair.

In the whir of his office, the manager said, "Shut the door, Johnny."

Whether the manager had arranged to fire me or fuck me, I didn't care at this point. With the virus in place, nothing else mattered.

"First of all," the manager started, "you might want to ask Danny to stop telling salacious jokes at work. Laughing at them could even get *you* into trouble."

I looked surprised and said, "He tells jokes like that all the time. Now that you mention it, I think he might be racist. And lately he's been acting a little...oh, I don't know."

The manger encouraged me, "Go ahead. How has he been acting?"

"Well...he's been a little strange at work. He's been absent a lot, and when he is here, he only works half as hard as he normally does, which is like trying to divide zero by half. And, he makes very negative remarks on Beamer as a company. Disaffection, yes, that's the word. One day he was looking at a white supremacy website. He even threatened to beat me up once, menacing me with the fact that he's a black belt in karate."

The manager pursed his lips while he wrote down all that I told him. "Goodness! I'd better keep an eye on him. We don't need unstable types in this department. I appreciate your honesty, Johnny."

"Anytime."

The manager leaned back in his chair and folded his arms. "It's that time of year again, Johnny. Time for individual performance reviews. Crunch-time, so to speak. Things haven't been as good on the fiscal end this year, so Beamer has gotten lean and mean in cutting costs wherever possible. I've had to make a lot of tough decisions this year in these performance reviews, but the only option Beamer has is to keep the best employees and depart with the lesser performers."

"Yes, indeed. What a pity it is," I mocked, and quibbled my finger on my lip.

"It is," the manager went on, "You're right about that..." Before continuing the manager paused briefly with an artificial somber face, as if saying a prayer for fallen Beamer comrades. Then his face and moustache returned to normal. "The reason I'm telling you this is that...Johnny, I've decided that you as an employee can realize your potential better somewhere else. In other ways than debugging, so I've decided to promote you."

"Oh good heavens," I fibbed, "That is wonderful news!"

"We want to keep you here, Johnny, so you don't go looking elsewhere for higher compensation. In addition to higher pay, you will be offered stock options and the highest bonus possible for the year."

"I'm thrilled. You have made my day, sir," I stood up and grabbed the manager's hand with both of my hands, shaking his arm with vigor.

"I'll e-mail the details to you, Johnny. Keep up the good work!"

"Ok, thank you. I will, sir. Can I go home for the day then...you know...to celebrate?"

"Absolutely!" the manager beamed. "Why not? You've earned it."

"Goodbye then!" I said, stepping into the hallway.

"Wait, Johnny - there is one more thing." He paused and smiled coyly. His moustache quivered. He said, "How 'bout them Green Bay Packers?"

I tilted my head and smiled. "How a-bout them Vikings!"

/* How one morning I found myself stuck in bed. */

Nothing pleased me more than nothing. I went home to lay on my living room carpet and slobber. I felt, looked, and probably even smelled like a spent shotgun shell. This is burnout.

In the coming weeks, the bed became harder to roll out of, with the chores of the day ahead feeling like Sisyphean tasks, Herculean, or, no – I felt like Sylvia Plath (but my oven was electric instead of gas). No matter how many times I rolled out of bed, the duress of knowing I had to do it again tomorrow became a millstone around my neck, until one day, after the seventh snooze, I failed to find the energy to push the snooze button on the alarm clock again.

The alarm was set to white noise, radio-static, which made the dawn of my consciousness muzzy. My eyes were scared to open, hoping rather to stay grounded in false sleep, pretending that the conscious world of Beamer was a dreamscape. I coveted the lives of comatose hospital patients who lived entirely in transient sleep. But I knew that sooner or later, the day would permeate my eyelids, no matter how uninvited, and my eyes would open. Slowly the image of my bedroom registered, forcing the disruption of peace.

When I sat up, I turned my feet to the unkempt carpet still laden with the syrup-bile tar pit from the day Katya left me. I sat up and looked into the mirror that faced my bed. A reflection of an exhausted personality talked at me.

My reflection jeeved at me in fluent poppycock: "Pray tell me, sir, of the gifts of your sensory perception. This mirror I'm inside measures nothing but geometry and hue; it's a simple tool of light, really, not suited to explain or construe. I only have your image built by the geometry of light, without the luxury of knowing the environment or the history to which you are privy. I wonder how this appearance you adorn has become you, since not long ago you looked so different. Tell me now: is the room freezing your skin to this level of paleness, or have your dreams scared you white? Are you on a fast, perhaps, and I've caught you at a fortnight? Pardon my prying, but I can't help but ask; is that a wrinkle laced on your cheek? I'd guess it to be a laugh line, but not with that frown you often wear. I would, in fact, call the line more of a crease. And do you see where the crease travels north to your disheveled waves of hair, where a pond of gray has formed over your ear? You must have spilled some paint, or been sprayed with dust, for the number of years you've lived is too short for such a taint. And can you see the sacks beneath your once deep and dark brown eyes? It seems the brown dye has bled south and turned the fertile skin to drought red, and is surrounded by a pallor that looks sown with salt. Tell me, what is it exactly that I'm looking at? Is that your head or an under-ripe prickly peach?" Then the voice of my reflection went silent.

I flopped a hand to scratch my prickly peach-head, pondering how to go any further, wondering how the day could possibly improve from this lackluster moment, wondering where would the energy come from to squeeze out enough calories to stand up and carry my prickly peach far enough to reach a sink, where I could drag a razor over the stubble of my face, then rinse the skin free of the aloe chemical besot, then whitewash the enamel of my incisors with a bristled device. I wondered how after that I could lumber down the long hall to the cupboard, pull open the door, reach inside for a bowl, shut the cupboard door, set the bowl down, select the proper drawer handle and pull, select a single spoon at rest among the other spoons, close the drawer to a safe position, then turn my body to face the refrigerator, reach upward to pull the freezer handle, withstand the adjustment of body temperature as the thermally mastered air erected goosebumps to make me shiver, then move my hand using muscular-skeletal contractions to lift a container holding several kilograms of ice cream, hoist the pail by the swinging handle that bobbed back and forth when carried through thin air, place the ice cream pail on the countertop near the already prepared bowl & spoon ensemble, use my fingers as a crude wedge to pry off the protective ice cream cover so I could mine chunks of a frozen material using nothing but a blunt spoon (causing my central nervous system to activate millions of neurons and nerve endings to have my eyes notify my hands what and how much ice cream I had scooped so I would know when to stop)...and then to actually eat the ice cream and clean up the tools and utensils used in the process...all so that I could arrive at work before noon? Impossible.

I scratched my prickly peach again, and then fell flat, defeated after one too many mornings. A fly crawled on the window near my bed, close enough that my heavy arm could reach the glass. The fly buzzed wildly as he bounced up and down against the window pane, trying to escape. I placed my finger next to the fly, forcing his desperate bounce to start again. He buzzed and beat his body on the pane. The little fly entertained me for some time, as I followed him around with my index finger, tormenting him. Every time he saw my finger nearing, he burst into a dribble, buzzing helplessly, almost as if he didn't realize how easy his escape from my finger really was. All he had to do was fly away from the window. Instead he tortured himself with the same routine and self-abuse. From flat on my back, I enjoyed exploiting the insect's stubborn lack of reason and innate masochism.

Ignorance is bliss; a greater bliss than solitude. I envied the fly. I wished to devolve into an insect or winged beast with a tiny brain. I wished to fall to the earth gracefully like a bird.

There was only one thing to do that day, and that was to go skydiving.

/* How I wound up skydiving with what appeared to be a faulty canopy. */

I flung my body out of bed in a burst, dressed, grabbed $2,000 in cash I had wadded up in a drawer, and dashed outside to my car. Driving recklessly, I headed east to God's country: Wisconsin. Using my cell phone and operator assistance, I connected with a skydiving agency. A weary voice answered the phone.

"Hello?"

"Hi, I'm calling to go skydiving."

"We only offer lessons on Saturdays."

"How about a lesson for one thousand dollars?"

"What? Are you serious, man?"

"Not enough? How about two thousand dollars?"

"Dude, it's a deal. I'll just ah...see if I can find a pilot."

I said, "You drive a hard bargain. I'm on my way."

I dialed my manager at work, to let him know I wouldn't make it to our scheduled meeting that day. The office whir crept over the phone line.

"Are you ok?" he lilted.

"I'm going skydiving in Wisconsin," I lilted in reply. "See you tomorrow maybe."

"Ah, yes! Skydiving in Packer-land. I'll make a note of it. Have fun!"

I didn't hang up. I chucked the phone out the window of the moving car, killing the whir once and for all, and I put the pedal to the floor.

The parking lot at the airfield was empty. From the looks of the run-down shack and the sign, the place appeared deserted. I jumped out of the car and peered into a window of the dingy little shack and saw a the telltale leftovers of a wild party. In the center of the room dangled a single dirty light bulb. In the far corner, a man in his early twenties slowly packed a parachute into a sack. I tapped on the window. He looked up.

"Hola, hombre!" he shouted, although he was as Spanish as Columbus. "Are you the dude that called from the road? You must have drove a long way."

"I did. Is that my parachute?"

"If you want. But for two thousand bucks, you can use my parachute, and I'll use this old one here. Why the rush to skydive, man?"

The dude pushed hair out his eyes and waited for me to reply.

"Because," I said, "anything on earth...anything in heaven or hell...is better than going into Beamer for another day of programming shitboxes."

"Woah," he said, "that's hardcore angst, man."

I said, "I need to let my container air out, know what I mean?"

"Oh, for sure, I know what you mean."

"I want the earth to be my only container today. The earth and the other cosmic containers outside of the earth."

The dude smiled, "Sweet. That's a sweet a reason, dude. Dude, I normally would never let any new person skydive without my boss around..."

I lied, delving into my HTML Cowboy pseudo-knowledge, "Oh, I've skydived lots of times. I have my 82nd

Airborne patch at home. I'm an official five-jump-chump. Army. Fort Sumter."

"Oh yeah, huh? That's cool. Well, then I doubt if my boss would care. Plus, if I split the money with him, he definitely won't mind, know what I mean, man? I could so use some extra scratch right now."

I licked my thumb and pulled out my wad of cash. I said, "Perfect. I need to get rid of some cash anyway. Here you go - one hunderd, two hunderd, three hunderd, four funderd, five hunderd, six hundred..."

"Damn, man, you are liquid. Do you want a receipt or something?"

"Absolutely not."

The pilot showed up, buzzing the strip in front of the shack in his little jalopy airplane. He landed and came inside to see who the urgency of flight was for. The 'dude' handed the pilot a few hundred dollar bills, and the pilot turned right back around and waited in the airplane for us.

The dude helped me get into his jumpsuit and parachute rig and he put on an old brown painter's outfit. He asked me if I wanted a walkie-talkie so that I could converse with him while I was in the air in case something went wrong or if I needed landing guidance. I declined the offer, telling him that I still remembered how to skydive from old Staff Sergeant Hooever.

I asked, "You pull the right-side ripcord first, right?"

The dude laughed and said, "You're joshin' me, right?"

"Yeah. Yeah," I smiled confidently, "I'm just joshin' ya."

Based on his response, I decided to pull the left-hand ripcord first, entirely unsure of myself, but enjoying the adventure of not knowing. I realized that I should have spent more time as an HTML Cowboy on the topic of skydiving.

The pilot opened up the engine a few thousand RPM's, increasing the sound and intensity of the moment. The electric air circled me as I walked to the crusty little airplane. The dude walked alongside me. Before we crawled into the tiny fuselage, the dude pulled out five pesticide bottles that read "Atrazine" on the label.

The dude said, "Our pilot also works as a crop duster on the side."

"Perfect!" I said.

I crawled inside, feeling butterflies tickling my stomach. The dude told the pilot to climb to ten thousand feet. The pilot nodded and took off.

Dude said, "Forty seconds of free fall should air out your container, huh, man?"

Hearing those words, I changed my mind and yearned to be sitting safely in the Shittoon, in the warmth of Beamerdom. But I knew the time had passed for stooling and wiping and debugging. The little plane made wide circles in the air as it climbed to ten thousand feet. Due to the engine noise the dude kept yelling at me, saying nerve-wracking comments like, "No matter how many times I jump, I still feel scared as a baby on the way up. And when the door opens, I nearly lose all courage, but I'm always able to jump because, let's face it, what's the alternative? To go back to the ground like a pussy that couldn't take the plunge? I'd rather die than be a chicken."

Next the dude took out his one-hitter named Lulu, as he called it. He screwed the end of the one-hitter into a little wooden box, then pulled Lulu out and lit one end like a cigarette. He inhaled intensely, and said to me as if he was choking, "D-ya' want some Lulu? This will definitely let you out of your container. Way out. This stuff will have you skydiving even when you are back on the ground." He coughed and exhaled a puff of violet smoke. I obliged his offer and inhaled as deep as I could, thinking that I may as well get a full two thousand dollars worth out of the experience.

"Ok, that's ten thousand feet," yelled the pilot, "and you are over the drop zone, good to go."

"Whoo-eeee!" shrieked the dude, as he crouched into a baseball catcher's stance and waddled toward the door. He shoved the door open so that nothing but one step forward stood between us and blank space. With the door open, the engine blared intensely.

Dude yelled, "DO YOU WANT TO JUMP FIRST OR SHOULD I?"

"YOU GO AHEAD," I yelled, with my bowels puckered tight.

He smiled. "Then, adios, amigo." With a little wave of his hand, the dude fell sideways, like a rock, right out of the door.

Gripping tight to a handle, I peeked over the edge of the airplane door, knowing that this airplane container could keep me safe. An abyss of air waited for me to become one of its items.

The pilot yelled, "If you don't go pretty soon I'll have to circle back over the drop zone."

I fingered the parachute gear on my chest, wondering which ripcord to pull, and when to pull it. My altimeter read 10,600 feet – two miles from the ground. I wondered when I would pull the ripcord. Should I pull the cord at eight thousand feet? Five thousand feet? Two thousand?

The pilot yelled, "C'mon pal, let's not make another loop here."

I gulped. There was nothing left to do. My lip quivered

as I looked at the pilot, "Adios, ami--"

--and the pilot banked hard right so that I was dumped out the open door--

Falling, twisting and turning in the wind, I yelled when my breath allowed me to be afraid. The altimeter spun quickly in increments of 100 feet per revolution of the needle. I flattened out into a belly-flop position, but soon flipped over again, screaming the whole loop. A strap on my goggles came loose and slapped me in the face violently until I stuffed the end of the strap into my jumpsuit collar. Finding the belly flop position impossible to maintain for long, I let my body turn whatever way the wind cared. The altimeter kept falling, now to 5,000 feet. I put my thumb into one of the ripcords, the left-side cord, then switched sides, I thumbed the right-side. Or was it the left side? Damn it. 4,000 feet. A crucible of stress and fear of death wrinkled me, and I knew that I might not live due to my rash ignorance. But what a way to go. 3,000 feet. At least, in death I would be uncontained. Yes, in death I might learn uncontainment at last. I felt the air rushing past me, or I past the air, rather.

The enlightening effect of Lulu kicked in and I wondered: "What is an item uncontained?"

Is an item uncontained useless?

Is it free?

Is it nothing?

Is it a state that can never be?

My goal, I realized, was to be uncontained. Falling I felt almost there. But really I was still utterly contained by many things. By the atmosphere and a subset of atmosphere. Once my chute opened the air would continually fill, overflow, and refill my parachute. My chute runneth over, upside down.

2,000 feet. Then to be uncontained cannot be a matter of geography or coordinates. It has to be where one feels least contained. Some people feel least contained inside a church, some in nature, some in drugs, some in software, some in political power, some in money, some in sex. Where do I feel least contained? Or rather, where do I feel most contained? I feel most contained in the office where the weight of the code squeezes the life out of my chest.

One thousand five hundred feet. But I can change my container. This is America. What am I complaining about...in the richest country in the world?

Perhaps I should stay for twenty-five years at Beamer so I can be rich, and then be free to play for the last twenty-five years of my life. Or maybe I could be free for all fifty years somehow.

But I am afraid to be poor. I have seen first-hand what a struggle it can be. My father advised against it. By my fear of being poor, I fear to pursue happiness. Then I may never be free. Both poor and rich people can love, dance, and sleep the same.

1,000 feet. I've waited too long.

Rolling the dice, I pulled the right-side ripcord and a parachute deployed, much to my relief. However, the canopy did not seem fully opened. A piece of canvas at the bottom didn't slide upward, like in pictures I'd seen on the internet. Or was the canvas supposed to slide upward on the chute at all? I guessed like a fool, using terminology I had learned from a website.

I pulled on the toggle lines hoping to see an improvement in the parachute, not that I really knew whether the chute worked properly to begin with. When I looked up, something seemed wrong. The symmetry or aesthetic failed me. And Death neared. I looked to the horizon to see Death ride across the sky to smote my confused life.

But on the horizon all I saw was the ending of the day. The close of another day of life coming as the sun fell down with me. Stealth is the night. It comes in closure, in peace with no promises, gradually sneaking up on the tree lines and pushing the shadows out from underneath until the dark creeps up our feet, then to our thighs, then our eyes so we are blind again. People like me fail to know when to go inside for the day. We stay outside to play, dreaming that our games will never end. I am a hopeless night wanderer. A solitary idiot still learning the way. Hopelessly in love with Katya but she was gone. Then I felt a clean feeling come over me, like a little boy feels when his mother wipes his face. I wanted to live in the worst way.

I groped at the cables of my faulty parachute, jerking it from side to side in agony, and yelled out to the earth, "If this is my last moment and I have only one more sentence to say, then it is: I love you, Katya! Only with you do I feel uncontained and free!"

The altimeter read 500 feet.

Then I thought, what if the altimeter is not calibrated correctly, and I really only have a few seconds to live? I looked straight down. The ground rushed towards me. Or it didn't. In the air, the depth perception of the human eye plays tricks, so I didn't know how close to the earth I really was. I slapped at the plastic face of the altimeter, hoping to jar the needle to the correct altitude. I looked at my watch to note the time of my death but I noticed the date instead.

Danny's birthday.

The virus had executed at noon.

On the ground, the skydive dude detached his parachute from his body and started waving his hands in a manic motion, trying to convey something to me. I waved at him and put up my hands as if to say, "What, me? Worry?" He ran over to a large, inflated windsock on a pole. He tugged at the windsock showing me the direction of the wind, then he circled his finger wide in the air. He kept circling his finger in the air, but I shook my head in wonder, accepting my certain death as final.

Suddenly I noticed a flurry of dust near the skydiving shack, where three police squad cars came rumbling into the gravel parking lot. The red and blue lights of the squad cars twirled, radiating a rather beautiful multimedia display of wind-muted sound and light given my height and distance from the parking lot, not to mention Lulu's distortion of my senses. The police officers stepped out of the squad cars, and walked toward the drop zone. I must have been negligent.

Then the earth rose up to meet me, quickly, and I stiffened my legs to land in a little garden, and when I hit, the last sound I heard was both of my femur bones snapping in half and that's when I said, fast as a cursor blink: first of all, Katya, this is not a suicide note.

Visit StoneGarden.Net Publishing Online!

You can find us at: www.stonegarden.net, the book shop is available from: http://bookshop.stonegarden.net.

News and Upcoming Titles

New titles and reader favorites are featured each month, along with information on our upcoming titles.

Author Info

Author bios, blogs and links to their personal websites.

Contests and Other Fun Stuff

Web forum to keep in touch with your favorite authors, autographed copies and more!

An Exciting New Sci-Fi Talent!
Michael Prokop

Starship Moonhawk

🞎 Inside Outsider (0-9765426-0-9-$5.99 US)

When trouble starts on a remote outpost, the Moonhawk and her crew are called out to investigate, but all is not as it seems when the Outsiders are involved. Are they acting alone, or are they receiving help from the Alliance's arch nemesis: The Crysallian Collective?

Discover who is the **Inside Outsider**

StoneGarden.Net Publishing

3851 Cottonwood Dr., Danville, CA   94506

Please send me the **StoneGarden.net Publishing** book I have checked above. I am enclosing $_____ (check, money order for US residents only, VISA and Mastercard accepted—no currency or COD's). Please include the list price plus $3 per order to cover handling costs ($5 outside of the US). Prices and numbers are subject to change without notice. (Prices slightly higher in Canada.)

Name:_____

Address:_____

City:_____State:_____Zip:_____Country:_____

VISA/Mastercard:_____

Exp. Date and CVS Code:_____ /_____

Please allow 4-6 weeks for delivery.

Printed in the United States
72693LV00001B/64